D0827872

Blaze

Dear Reader,

I'll admit it; I do read celebrity gossip and showbiz news and there are several actors whose careers I have followed over the years. Over time, most of these Hollywood hotties have found their own happily-ever-afters and have tied the knot, dropping off the list of eligible celebrity bachelors. But then there are those few who, despite being drop-dead gorgeous, talented and personable, remain single. So that got me thinking....

What if one of these stars had a youthful first love that he'd never forgotten? Or what if he'd done something really crazy, like secretly eloped with her, only to have the relationship fall apart? And what if, years later, his first love reappeared in his life?

And so Graeme and Lara's story was born. He's jaded and disillusioned, but he's never forgotten sweet, idealistic Lara. She wants to finally put him in her past and move on with her life. After all, what they had couldn't possibly have been *that* good, right?

I hope you enjoy reading their story. I love hearing from readers, so please drop me a note at karenefoley@comcast.net.

Hugs,

Karen

Karen Foley

HOLD ON TO THE NIGHTS

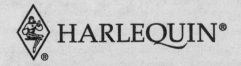

HARLEQUIN®

TORONTO • NEW YORK • LONDON
AMSTERDAM • PARIS • SYDNEY • HAMBURG
STOCKHOLM • ATHENS • TOKYO • MILAN • MADRID
PRAGUE • WARSAW • BUDAPEST • AUCKLAND

Recycling programs
for this product may
not exist in your area.

ISBN-13: 978-0-373-79508-6

HOLD ON TO THE NIGHTS

Books by Karen Foley

HARLEQUIN BLAZE
353—FLYBOY
422—OVERNIGHT SENSATION
451—ABLE-BODIED

For Gerry.

And for Brenda,
the best editor a girl could ask for.

Prologue

JOSIE HEARD the rumble of the delivery truck when it arrived. Leaning over the counter, she peered through the display window with its colorful exhibit of costumed mannequins, toward the street, where a large van had pulled up to the curb. She'd been eyeballing Tom, the delivery guy, for two months now, and today she was finally going to let him know she was interested.

Stepping back from the window, Josie glanced down at the costume she'd chosen. The costume shop, Dressed to Thrill, wasn't big, but what space they did have was packed with variety. In the end, she'd selected a slave-girl getup, complete with collar and chain. It was a high-end reproduction of the same outfit Princess Leia had worn in *Return of the Jedi,* after she'd been captured by Jabba the Hutt and added to his harem.

The bells over the door tinkled, and a gust of cool, autumn air caused goose bumps to rise on her bare flesh.

"Hi, Tom. I've been waiting for you."

"Hey, Josie," he said, his eyes running over her as he brought the two-wheeled dolly to a stop. "Wow. That's, uh, quite the outfit you're wearing."

Josie leaned close to him as she signed the receipt for the cartons of costumes and accessories. "Like it?"

He swallowed hard. "It looks great on you."

"So," she purred, "how've you been? It's been a while since you've...*delivered*."

Tom's neck and ears turned ruddy. "Yeah," he agreed with an uneasy laugh. "It's been a while."

Josie edged even closer, prepared to really crank up the heat, when his cell phone rang. He smiled apologetically before he reached for the small phone at his hip. Turning away, he spoke into the receiver. "Well, hello there, sweetie," he crooned.

Sweetie? Josie stared at him in dismay before walking quickly back to the reception counter where a computer beeped loudly, indicating an online order had just arrived. She automatically opened the e-mail request, but her eyes were on Tom as he bent his head and spoke quietly into the phone. The thought that he might be involved with somebody hadn't crossed her mind, not when he looked at her as if he was starving and she was an all-you-can-eat buffet. She wanted to howl with frustration at the unfairness of it all. Just when she was getting up the courage to finally put the moves on him.

With one eye on Tom, Josie scanned the online order from a woman right here in Chicago named Lara Whitfield. She was requesting any costume related to the popular sci-fi television series, *Galaxy's End*. Josie was a huge fan of the hit show, which starred sexy Scottish actor, Graeme Hamilton. She read the short note that Lara Whitfield had included at the bottom of her order.

I'm attending a *Galaxy's End* fan festival in two days, so need this shipped overnight express. I'd prefer something all-concealing, like the shaman costume.

A fan festival, huh? Josie snorted, envisioning a ballroom filled with middle-aged, overweight women, all clamoring for a kiss or an autograph from the famed actor. Lara Whitfield obviously needed a life. It was one thing to crush on a delivery guy; it was another thing altogether to crush on a Hollywood celebrity.

One thing was certain, however; Lara Whitfield wouldn't get so much as a second glance from *any* guy if she was disguised as the *Galaxy's End* shaman. That particular costume was more concealing than a burka. Besides which, they were running low on stock, having just gotten through the Halloween rush. Josie was pretty sure they were sold out of *Galaxy's End* costumes.

A quick electronic query of the shop's inventory confirmed her suspicions. Worse, when she performed a query for alternative costumes, the computer returned a picture of the very same *Star Wars* slave-girl outfit that Josie wore right now.

Across the shop, Tom finished his conversation and turned back to Josie. She gave him a polite smile, refusing to be misled by the appreciation in his eyes. "Thanks, Tom," she said airily, and turned back to the computer, pretending to be absorbed in the online order. "I'll see you next time."

She sensed his confusion, but didn't look at him again. When the door closed behind him, her shoulders slumped. Drawing in a fortifying breath, she concentrated on the order. Too bad the customer had asked for something that concealed rather than revealed; Josie was certain the slave-girl getup would garner more attention than the woman had ever had in her life and she wanted nothing more than to get rid of the exotic costume. Having it in the shop was a humiliating reminder of her failure with Tom. She was in the middle of responding that they had no costumes available, when her fingers paused over the keyboard.

Why *couldn't* she send Lara Whitfield the slave-girl costume? Sure, it was revealing, but the size was right. She'd even throw in a gorgeous, wrought-gold mask that would match the metal bikini and completely disguise her face, for free. What did it matter that it was a *Star Wars* costume and not a *Galaxy's End* costume? They were both sci-fi space flicks, right? Besides, she'd be doing the poor woman a favor. Nobody would even notice her in the shaman's voluminous robes, but the slave-girl getup was guaranteed to turn heads. And just to make sure the customer didn't complain *too* much, she'd give it to her at a twenty-five percent discount. Combined with the free mask, it was more than a bargain; it was a steal.

With a grim smile, Josie typed in the stock number for the slave-girl costume and completed the order. Pushing back from the counter, she made her way to the stockroom to remove and package the costume. She refused to think about how the customer would react when she opened the parcel and realized she'd received the wrong item. Josie had screwed up orders before, but never deliberately. She told herself she had the customer's best interests in mind. She just hoped the costume would bring Lara Whitfield better luck than it had brought her.

1

LARA WHITFIELD paced her hotel room, uncertain what to do now that she was actually here in Las Vegas, possibly in the very same hotel as *him*. She'd never attended a celebrity fan festival before, and wasn't certain what to expect. Certainly not the throngs of women she'd encountered in the hotel lobby, who gushed and quivered with excitement over the fact that Graeme Hamilton would be here, in the flesh.

Even after following his meteoric career, Lara found herself stunned by the enormity of his appeal. For all intents and purposes, he hadn't existed as a public figure until he was cast as the sexy bad-boy character, Kip Corrigan, in the hit television series *Galaxy's End*. The pilot episode had aired two years earlier and, seemingly overnight, every woman in America wanted him. Based on the chaotic scene in the hotel lobby, Lara was convinced that every last one had traveled to the fan festival in the hopes of seeing him.

Her cell phone rang, startling her. Digging into her purse, she pulled it out and glanced at the display, smiling ruefully when she saw the number. She'd forgotten to call Val when she'd arrived at the hotel. Her college roommate and best friend, Valerie was worse than any mother. Now Lara flipped the phone open, knowing she was going to get an earful.

"Hi, Val," she said, squinting. "I, um, made it here safely."

"Uh-huh," came the exasperated voice on the other end. "I've only been worried half out of my head, wondering if you were okay."

Lara walked over to the window and pushed aside the curtain. Below her, the Las Vegas strip teemed with activity. "I'm fine. I don't know why you worry about me so much."

Val made a tsking sound. "Maybe because you have your head in the clouds most of the time. I wouldn't have been at all surprised if you'd gotten on the wrong flight and ended up in Europe somewhere."

"No, I'm definitely here in Las Vegas." Lara dropped the curtain. "I wish you had come with me. It feels... strange to be here by myself."

"Sorry, kiddo," Val said sympathetically. "But I think you were right—this is something you need to do on your own. Besides, who would help Christopher run the theater program if we were both in Las Vegas?"

Lara pushed down the pang of guilt she felt at the mention of the program, reminding herself that she would be gone for less than a week, hardly enough time for the children to miss her.

Since she'd been a small child, Lara had wanted to be involved in the theater. Her parents had divorced when she was just four, and her father had moved to Washington, D.C., to pursue a political career. Lara had grown up on her mother's estate on the outskirts of Chicago, while her mother had spent most of her time pursuing and capturing husbands number two, three and four.

Lara's childhood visits with her father had been filled with parties and soirées where she'd either been stuck in a corner and forgotten, or left in his cavernous apartment with the housekeeper.

Alone and lonely, she had imagined herself as a princess locked away in a forbidden castle with only fairy creatures to keep her company. Surrounded by a host of imaginary friends, she probably had seemed an odd and pitiable child, but her make-believe world had been very real to her.

Eventually, she'd put her imagination to good use, obtaining a degree in theater arts and writing. While she resisted using her family's influential connections, she hadn't been above tapping into the substantial trust fund her father had set up for her to open a small drama school for underprivileged children on Chicago's west side. If anyone needed to escape the harsh realities of life, even for a few hours each day, it was the children who attended the inner-city theater program.

The nonprofit program only operated in the afternoons and during weekends, so Lara also did some freelance writing for several different magazines. The money wasn't great, but it paid her bills. The theater program, however, was where she invested most of her time and energy.

Christopher had been her screenwriting professor in college and when he'd heard about her venture, had expressed an interest in getting involved. They had worked together for more than six months before he'd finally asked her for a date, and even then Lara's first reaction had been to refuse him. He'd persisted, however, and finally she had acknowledged that unless she made some drastic personal changes, she risked going through life alone, with only her imagination and her memories to keep her company. The fourth time that Christopher had asked her out, she'd accepted.

He was smart and sweet, and if he didn't make her blood heat and her body throb with need, she was mature enough to realize that he was still a good catch.

A great catch.

Lara knew that at the slightest indication from her, he'd take their relationship to the next level. But no matter how much she told herself she wanted that, as well, she still held a part of herself back. She'd finally acknowledged that she'd subconsciously been hanging on to her memories of Graeme, reliving the past through her erotic stories.

Until she put Graeme behind her and stopped writing fan fiction about him, under the guise of writing about Kip Corrigan, she would never truly be over him. And until she was over Graeme, she couldn't begin a meaningful relationship with Christopher.

"You didn't tell him I was here, did you?" She asked Valerie.

She didn't want to think about how Christopher might react if he knew she was spending the next few days in Las Vegas. Alone. At a sci-fi fan festival. He'd think she'd completely lost her mind.

"Relax, of course not," her friend replied. "I confirmed what you told him—that you needed some time by yourself after your father's death. He totally believes that you're at your mother's beach house on the Outer Banks, doing some deep meditation on the meaning of life."

"You said that?"

"Well, except for the deep meditation. But he knows how much your dad's death upset you, especially considering you hadn't really reconciled with him before he died. He understands that you need some time."

Lara blew out a hard breath, hating the deception, but feeling as if she hadn't had any other choice. "Okay, thanks. And thanks, too, for covering for me at the theater for the next couple of days. Make sure you give Alayna an extra hug from me, okay? And tell her I'll definitely be back in time to see her performance. I don't think she believed me when I said I'd only be gone for a few days."

"I will. I know you have a soft spot for her, and she's going to miss you like crazy, poor little thing." There was a brief silence while they both thought of the tiny girl with the enormous eyes, whose mother had been killed in a random shooting, an innocent victim who had been in the wrong place at the wrong time. Since the incident, Alayna had become very attached to Lara, unwilling to leave her side at the theater.

The kids were rehearsing a stage performance of *The Wizard of Oz,* and nine-year old Alayna had the role of one of the Munchkins. Lara knew how nervous the little girl was, and had promised to be at the performance, just three weeks away, to cheer her on.

"So, have you seen him yet?"

Lara knew she referred to Graeme. "No. I haven't even left my room yet." She shuddered. "You should see how many people are here, Val. I swear, there must be thousands. I'm not sure if I can do this."

"Lara, you have to." Val's voice was firm. "He deserves to know the truth."

"I know. It's just..." Lara's voice grew small. "All

these years, I've imagined him a certain way. What if he's changed?"

"We all change. Trust me, you've changed, too, Lara. In fact, he might not even recognize you, that's how much you've changed in the past five years."

Lara laughed. "I'm not sure about that."

"Oh, I am," Val said, and Lara could hear the smile in her voice. "When I first met you, you were withdrawn to the point of being backward."

"I was reserved," Lara said primly. "And heartbroken."

"Uh-huh. My point exactly. And look at you now— teaching drama to a bunch of underprivileged kids, writing erotic fan fiction on the Internet, and dating your former professor who just happens to be the hottest faculty member on campus. I'd say you've come a long way, baby."

Lara gave a helpless laugh. Christopher was hot? Sure, he was good-looking in an artsy, academic way, with his shaggy hair and easy smile, but in the months that they'd been dating, Lara had never once thought of him as *hot*.

"He is cute," she acknowledged. "But as far as the erotic fiction goes…I've actually decided to give it up."

There was a stunned silence. *"What?"*

Lara sat on the edge of the desk and her hand drifted to the stack of conference brochures that she'd brought with her from Chicago. Sifting through the pile, Lara withdrew a recent issue of *People* magazine. Staring back at her from the glossy front cover was a full-page photo of Graeme Hamilton. His blue-green eyes gazed warmly at her, and his lips curved in the vaguest suggestion of a smile, providing just a hint of the deep dimples that had endeared him to millions of female fans.

"I can't keep doing it, Val. To my readers, the stories are just steamy tales about the *Galaxy's End* characters, but I know they're more than that." She stared at the cover of the magazine. "I know they're really my own fantasies about Graeme, and they're not healthy. If I really want to put him in my past and move on with my future, then I need to stop writing about him. About Kip."

The photograph of him was so clear that Lara could see the individual stubble of whiskers on his jaw. Tiny laugh lines splayed out from the corners of his eyes and for a moment, Lara's heart contracted painfully. She ran her fingers over the image. Beneath her hand, she could almost feel the rough velvet of his cropped hair.

"I understand how you feel, Lara, I do," Val said, her voice sympathetic. "But your stories have such a huge following. I checked your stats this morning and the story that you posted last night has already received more than ten thousand hits. Ten thousand hits in just one day, Lara! That's completely crazy, you know that, right? I don't think you have any idea how popular your stories on these Web sites are."

"Well, maybe I'll find another character to focus on, then. But I can't keep writing about Kip Corrigan. He's too real to me, and it brings back too many memories. I need to find something else to write about." Lara glanced at her watch. "Listen, Val, I have to go. The masquerade ball is starting soon. If I'm really going to do this, then I should probably go scope out the situation first."

"Okay. Call me. Anytime, for any reason. Promise?"

"I promise. I'll call you as soon as I get back to the room."

She hung up and placed the phone on the table. She and Valerie had been roommates since their first year of college and they were closer than most sisters. After they'd graduated, they'd continued to share an apartment. Valerie knew all Lara's secrets, including her reasons for attending the fan festival.

Lara looked again at the magazine she held in her hand. The caption beneath the photo read, "Graeme Hamilton—Sexy and Single!" Lara groaned. Sexy? Most definitely. Single? Most definitely not.

Should she venture down to the convention and join the hordes of other women all clamoring to get a glimpse of the hot Hollywood stud, or bide her time until she could get him alone? Lara glanced at her watch. If she wanted to join the festivities, she'd need first to slip into the *Galaxy's End* costume that she'd brought with her. She'd specifically ordered a costume that would conceal her identity and allow her to blend in with the crowd. There was no way she wanted Graeme to recognize her before she was ready. She had a plan for how their encounter would unfold, and it didn't include crowds of partygoers.

Even now, after two weeks, she still couldn't quite accept the chain of events that had brought her to the second annual *Galaxy's End* fan festival. Her gaze slid reluctantly to the sheath of legal documents that she had carried with her from Chicago to Las Vegas. They lay on the polished surface of the desk looking harmless enough, but Lara knew better. Those seemingly innocent papers had turned her safe, orderly world upside down.

"Damn, damn, damn," she muttered under her breath, and, giving into temptation, snatched up the letter that lay folded on top of the documents.

Most people came to Las Vegas for a quick wedding. She'd come for a quick divorce, or at least a quick signature on the divorce papers that she'd brought with her. The kicker was, the guy in question didn't even realize he was still married. Each time Lara tried to envision how he might react to that little tidbit, she had a full-blown panic attack.

She could have let her lawyer handle the nasty job of breaking the news to him, but she felt strongly that this was something she should do. She was a true glutton for punishment.

Sinking into the upholstered chair near the bed, Lara unfolded the letter and reread it, although she knew the contents by heart.

My darling Lara,

By the time you read this, I will be gone. I know that you despise me and I don't blame you, but please don't destroy this letter without first reading it through. I realize how difficult it was for you to visit me here at the hospice center today, but I am grateful to have seen you one last time before I go. For the first time in five years I have hope that you might eventually forgive me. Please know that what I did, I did because I loved you.

I wasn't the best of fathers, but I always wanted what was best for you. When you came to spend that summer with me in London, you were so grown-up. My hope was that we would

finally develop the kind of closeness that divorce
and distance had prevented, but I was too caught
up with my job.

I don't blame you for falling in love with that
boy. You always had a romantic heart, and you
thought he was your Prince Charming. But when
I discovered you had eloped with him, I did what
any father would do. Lara, you were just seventeen, and so naive. So sheltered. So trusting. He
had nothing to offer you. I knew, eventually, he
would break your heart and maybe even ruin your
life. So I put you on the next flight back to the
States and directed my lawyers to file the annulment papers, hoping that you would forget him.
I never guessed that I would lose you completely
in the process.

Yesterday, my deepest wish came true; you
finally came to see me and brought with you a
man whom I believe will love you and care for
you as you deserve. And now comes the most difficult part of this letter, for I have a confession to
make that will not endear me to you.

Your marriage to that boy was never annulled,
and my legal counsel informs me that despite my
best efforts, you are still legally wed. I didn't tell
you this earlier, because I thought that if you
knew, you might return to him. But now that you
are over him, and in the event that you plan to
marry again, you need to know the truth.

Please know that I only want your happiness.
Forgive me.
Your father,
Brent Whitfield

Lara dropped the letter into her lap and gave a small huff of laughter. Even at the end, her father had refused to call Graeme anything except *that boy*, as if by doing so he somehow diminished Graeme, both in his own mind and in Lara's eyes.

The news that she and Graeme were still married had hit her like a physical blow. She'd tried so hard to forget him, but the letter had brought all the emotions back in sharp relief—the longing for what might have been and the regrets for what would never be. Worse, she'd begun dreaming of Graeme again, and certain things had come back to her in startling clarity; his laugh, his smell...his taste.

Christopher had no idea she'd once been married, and Lara didn't relish telling him, even if that marriage had only lasted for two amazing, unforgettable nights. And if she was honest with herself, one of the reasons she was so reluctant to tell him was because a part of her realized that after five years, she shouldn't still be thinking about those two nights as often as she did.

Almost absently, Lara reached inside the open collar of her blouse and withdrew the small, round locket that lay nestled between her breasts. The silver was warm from her skin and she ran her finger over the delicate open-face filigree on the front, in the shape of a Celtic love knot. Helpless to resist and knowing she was a true glutton for punishment, she flicked the locket open.

On one side nestled a tiny photo of Graeme. His lips curved in the barest hint of a smile, but his eyes gleamed with suppressed laughter. Lara recalled the day the picture had been taken. She and Graeme had been walking along the Thames, arms wound around each other, when a peddler with a Polaroid had offered to take their photo for five pounds. Graeme hadn't been interested, but Lara had insisted. She'd wanted a photo of Graeme, and had tormented him until he'd finally capitulated. He'd encircled her in his arms with his chin resting on the top of her head.

Afterwards, he'd taken one look at the photo and declared it unfit to keep, although Lara hadn't missed how he gave the peddler ten pounds instead of five. She'd tried unsuccessfully to wrestle the photo from him until they were both breathless and laughing, and then the photo had been forgotten altogether.

Lara hadn't thought of the picture again until the day Graeme had given her the locket. He'd carefully snipped her face from the photo and had tucked it into one side of the locket, facing his picture. Lara had liked to think of their images, closed in the snug space, eternally kissing.

The locket had been her wedding gift from Graeme. Snapping the locket closed, Lara dropped it back beneath her blouse. Despite everything, she'd never been able to put the locket away. She wore it every day, like a talisman. It represented all the dreams she'd once had, the dreams that would never come true, thanks to her father. Even at his bedside, knowing he would die soon, she'd been unable to speak the words that she knew he'd longed to hear.

I forgive you.
You did the right thing.
I'm happy with the way my life has turned out.

After her father had died, Lara had come to the bitter realization that if her life hadn't turned out exactly as she'd hoped, then she had only herself to blame. She needed to forgive her father, cut her losses and move on. Getting Graeme to sign the divorce papers would be the first step.

Unzipping the outer compartment of her suitcase, Lara withdrew the bulky envelope that contained her costume. She'd ordered it just two days before leaving Chicago and had almost given up on receiving it in time to bring it with her to the convention. In fact, the UPS delivery truck had arrived at her townhouse at about the same time as her taxi had arrived to take her to the airport. She'd shoved the package into her suitcase and hadn't yet had an opportunity to look at the costume. Now she turned the lumpy packet over in her hands, noting the return address.

Dressed to Thrill, Chicago.

Lara had ordered costumes and accessories from the small shop before, but only to support the children's theater program. The nonprofit venture had a small staff and an even smaller budget, but the expressions on the kids' faces when they saw their new costumes made it worthwhile.

The envelope that contained her own costume was lumpy and hard in places, and Lara knew without opening the package that it didn't contain the shaman robe and hood that she'd requested. Of course, she hadn't specifically ordered the shaman costume. She'd indicated that any costume from the *Galaxy's End* television series would fit the bill, so long as it concealed her identity. What had the costume shop sent her instead? Turning the envelope over in her hand, Lara tore it open and dumped the contents onto the bed, ripping aside the lavender tissue paper.

What the—?

Lara gingerly picked up a piece of the costume and

inspected it. *No.* There was absolutely no freaking way she could wear this outfit. She'd asked for a costume that concealed her identity, one that would let her blend in with the crowd and enjoy the festival, secure in her own anonymity. Instead the costume shop had sent her…a skimpy slave-girl outfit!

And not just any slave-girl costume, either. It looked suspiciously like the one that Princess Leia had worn in the *Star Wars* movie.

Pushing aside the remnants of tissue paper, Lara spread the bits and pieces of the costume out on the flowered bedspread.

Yep, there was no doubt about it.

There in front of her was a perfect replica of the famous metal bikini with its wrought-gold top and bottom, the delicate, curved slave bracelets for her upper arms, the chunky slave collar and chain, and the tiny suede booties, cleverly designed with straps and Velcro to conform to any foot.

The only difference was that this ensemble also contained a gold mask, reminiscent of the Venetian Renaissance. Covering everything but the mouth and chin, the mask curved elegantly along the sides of the wearer's head and locked into place at the back.

How could the costume shop have made such a colossal mistake? There was no way she could wear this outfit, of course, and she felt a pang of regret that she would have to miss the masquerade ball.

Lara picked the mask up, turning it over in her hands and admiring it in spite of herself. Finely crafted, the mask was a work of art. How would it feel to wear such a gorgeous creation? Hesitating only briefly, she slid the mask over her face and fastened the closure. The lightweight metal felt cool against her skin.

When she peered at herself in the mirror, it was like looking at someone else. Even the familiarity of her own body, clad in figure-hugging jeans and a turquoise tank top, did little to dispel the sense that she was actually looking at an exotic stranger.

Entranced, she touched her fingers to her lips, exposed beneath the bottom edge of the gold face plate. She'd always considered her mouth too full, but now the gold mask framed her lips and emphasized their plumpness. They looked…hedonistic. Except for the glittering blue of her eyes behind the eye slits and the thick, red-gold hair that fell to her shoulders, she was unrecognizable.

Mysterious.

Lara glanced at the rest of the costume. Did she dare? She'd played a lot of dress-up games as a kid, but nothing like this. She'd never worn anything so risqué in her entire life. She'd asked for a costume that hid her identity so that she could size Graeme up without worrying that he might recognize her. But now, instead of being an anonymous observer, she'd stand out like a neon beacon. The costume was a scant step away from complete nudity. Not that she thought Graeme would recognize her even if she did decide to wear the costume.

What had Valerie said? That she'd changed in the last five years, so much so that even Graeme would have a hard time recognizing her. The mask would hide her features, and he wasn't even scheduled to make an appearance at the costume ball that was kicking off the convention tonight.

Maybe she did dare…

Eyeing the outfit warily, she pulled a single-serving bottle of white wine out of the minifridge. Before she'd even consider putting the costume on, she needed a little false courage. She twisted the cap off the bottle and took a deep swig, and then another. Quickly, before she could change her mind, she stripped out of her clothes and donned the costume. She had a moment's panic when her breasts refused to cooperate, and threatened to overspill the embossed cups of the bra. It was only after some jiggling and rearranging that she finally managed to subdue them.

Her silver locket lay nestled between her breasts, and she carefully removed it and placed it on her nightstand. Then she squeezed the bracelets around her upper arms and fastened the gold slave collar around her neck. A short length of chain hung from the front and lay cold and smooth against her breast.

For a long moment, Lara just stood and gazed into the mirror, hardly able to believe it was herself reflected there. She looked like a decadent offering, designed for a man's pleasure. Her skin gleamed pale and smooth beneath the bikini, and when she turned experimentally, the crimson cascade of fabric swirled and provided alluring glimpses of her legs. The brevity of the costume shocked her. The front and back of the metal bikini bottom were held together by gold loops, exposing her entire flank.

Turning to the side, Lara examined her profile, sucking her tummy in and then letting it out. She wasn't overweight, but there was a slight roundness to her belly that no amount of exercise or starvation could eliminate. But the reflection in the mirror wasn't of a pudgy girl, but a lushly curved woman. She'd always thought her breasts a bit too large for her small frame, but now the bra pushed them upward to a whole new fullness. They looked…sexy. *She* looked sexy. Erotic. Words that Lara would never have used to describe herself, but there was no question they applied to her now.

Lara gazed at her reflection, and a naughty thrill coursed through her. Did she dare attend tonight's costume ball like this? Just the thought of appearing in public dressed in such a salacious way brought a flush of color to her pale skin. She could have been a character straight from one of her own erotic stories. Which inspired another intriguing thought: how would the intergalactic outlaw, Kip Corrigan, react if he saw her?

Immediately, Lara's imagination surged, and she could almost anticipate how the fictional Kip would respond. He'd bend her backward over any available surface and feast on the bounty of exposed female flesh. Then he'd take his time removing the costume, piece by piece, until all that remained was the collar and length of chain around her neck. She could envision him wrapping the slender links around his fist and using the chain to hold her, while he plundered her sensitized breasts with his mouth.

Warm tendrils of excitement unfurled in Lara's womb, spreading outward and causing heat to build between her legs. She realized that her hands had drifted to the soft skin of her breasts just above the embossed bra, and her breathing had quickened. Beneath the lower edge of the mask, her lips were parted and damp, as if she anticipated a lover's kiss, and behind the eye slits, her irises shimmered hotly.

Closing her eyes, she shifted her internal focus slightly, imagining it was Graeme doing those things to her. The images in her head swam and then sharpened into stark relief, and she gasped softly. Instead of the fictional Kip, it was Graeme who stroked her heated flesh, all the while telling her in explicit, exciting detail what he intended to do to her, his Scottish burr more pronounced with his arousal.

In her mind's eye, he fastened his mouth around the aching bud of one nipple, drawing sharply on it. When she might have protested, he tugged gently on the chain, holding her in place. Meanwhile, his free hand skated along the silken skin of her abdomen until he found her core and stroked her slick center.

Lara's eyes flew open and she stared at her reflection, more aroused than she could recall being since...well, since the last time she'd had sex with Graeme, five years earlier. In the mirror, her breasts rose and fell in an agitated fashion, and her skin had taken on a warm, flushed glow. Her blood pulsed hot and quick through her veins, and her eyes were filled with sensual need.

With a soft groan of dismay, she picked up the small bottle of wine and drained the contents in one long swallow, then swiped her mouth with fingers that trembled.

She took a deep, calming breath, willing her pulse to slow down. What would Graeme think if he could see her now? In no way did she resemble the shy teenager she'd been when they'd first met. Lara hardly recognized herself.

She could do this; she could become the woman that Val had described; strong and sure of herself and of her own future. She told herself again that she'd moved on with her life; she had a job and a great guy who did care about her, and she couldn't—*wouldn't*—let herself believe there was anything left between her and Graeme.

They were strangers in every sense of the word.

And while millions of women would no doubt kill to marry Graeme, she knew that divorcing him would be the first smart thing she'd done in five years.

2

THE COSTUME BALL was already in full swing by the time Lara arrived at the ballroom. Under any other circumstances, she might have felt self-conscious about entering by herself, but then she caught a barely veiled expression of lust on the face of a passing waiter. That covert look told her that she looked good. Better than good—she looked delicious. With a smile, she accepted a pink-tinted pomegranate martini from a waiter who stood just inside the entrance, and took a hearty swallow, gasping as the alcohol burned its way down her throat. With her eyes watering, she stepped into the ballroom.

The lights had been dimmed and a large stage had been set up at one end, where a tuxedoed band played dinner music. Artificial trees, sparkling with minilights, lent a magical quality to the event. Three enormous movie screens had been placed at even intervals on the far wall, and clips from the show *Galaxy's End* played endlessly so that no matter where you looked, there was Graeme Hamilton in the role of deep-space convict Kip Corrigan.

For a moment, Lara stood in the doorway and just stared, transfixed by the Technicolor images. Would she ever get used to seeing his face? Would the day ever come when her heart didn't stop at the sight? Her life would be so much simpler if seeing him didn't affect her so much.

But it did.

With a soft groan, she gulped down the rest of the martini. She just had to keep remembering that the pictures she saw on the big screens weren't really Graeme. They were illusions, figments of somebody's imagination, the same way the stories she wrote were the embodiment of her own unfulfilled fantasies.

She was so done with fantasies.

Across the sea of linen-covered tables adorned with flowers and flickering candlelight, Lara could see a long buffet table where white-tuxedoed waitstaff served food to the masked and costumed ballgoers. On the parquet dance floor in front of the stage, couples dressed as various *Galaxy's End* characters danced together. The costumes were so impressive and so much like the ones from the actual show that Lara had a brief moment of unease. How badly did she stick out with her *Star Wars* getup? She shivered, aware that her scantily-clad body drew more than several appreciative glances from the men in the room.

Lara forced herself to move through the buffet line and then, plate in hand, searched for an empty seat among the crowded tables. She finally found one right next to the dance floor. The six women already seated there were dressed in identical costumes as Kip's on-screen love interest, a prison guard named Lily, despite the fact they were easily in their midfifties. They each gave her welcoming smiles, although Lara didn't miss how their eyes absorbed every detail of her own skimpy outfit.

Needing a little more false courage, she stopped a waiter as he passed near their table and snagged a second martini from his tray, although the first one seemed to be doing the trick. Even now, her limbs were feeling looser and the second drink didn't taste nearly as overpowering as the first had.

The woman closest to Lara turned to her and winked. "Now that's what I call a costume," she said.

Lara flushed behind the concealing mask, not sure if the woman was being sincere or sarcastic. Maybe she should have chosen a table of men. Maintaining an aura of sensuality was so much more difficult when surrounded by six matronly women, several of whom clearly disapproved of her revealing outfit, judging by their expressions.

"Thanks," she responded. "This isn't the costume I ordered, but by the time I received it, it was too late to get something else."

The woman on Lara's other side patted her arm reassuringly. "Don't think twice about it, hon. If I had a body like yours, I'd wear that costume, too. And that mask is absolutely fabulous."

Lara smiled gratefully at her. "So is this your first *Galaxy's End* convention?"

"Goodness, no," the woman laughed. "We were here last year, too. We've been Graeme Hamilton fans since day one." She indicated the other women at the table. "We call ourselves Hamilton's Hussies. Maybe you've heard of us? We practically started Graeme's fan club!"

Lara had heard of them. In fact, she was a frequent visitor to their Web site, dedicated to Graeme and to his career. She'd posted countless erotic stories about Kip Corrigan and the other *Galaxy's End* characters to the fan fiction page of the site, and had even exchanged e-mail correspondence with the Hussies under her screen name, Secret Lover.

But she didn't share any of this with the women at the table. Her stories were too personal to talk about with strangers, especially since they were based completely on Graeme Hamilton himself. She shivered to think how he would react if he could read her lusty tales. There was no doubt in her mind that he would recognize the main character as himself. Most of her stories were drawn directly from her own experiences with Graeme, right down to the dialogue.

Then there were her other stories…the ones based solely on her own imagination. With her writing, she was free to explore all her forbidden fantasies about Graeme, disguised as fan fiction about the *Galaxy's End* characters. In her stories, she could do anything, and she could have Graeme respond in any way she desired. She could relive every moment of that summer when she had first fallen in love with him. She could replay every heated second of their time at the Scottish inn when he'd aroused her to the point that she thought she might die from sheer pleasure, and then he'd shown her there was even more.

In her fan fiction, she enjoyed dominating him, forcing him to submit to her desires. But in the end, he would always wrest control back from her and then subject her to the most delicious torture.

"So you're a big Graeme Hamilton fan, huh?" she asked, picking at the cheese manicotti on her plate, and then mentally rolled her eyes at her own inane question.

"Aren't we all?" asked the second woman. Her short

brown hair was liberally sprinkled with gray, and there were lines around her eyes and mouth, but the excitement and anticipation in her eyes made her look like a schoolgirl. "I fell in love with him the first time I saw him in the pilot episode. I mean, how could any woman not fall head over heels for him, right?"

Lara avoided answering the question by taking a gulp of her martini. This was exactly why she'd been reluctant to attend the convention. Any minute now, they'd start gushing about Graeme's physical attributes and speculating about his love life. Was this what he had to endure every time he made a public appearance?

The woman on Lara's other side smiled knowingly as she speared a small roasted potato with her fork and popped it into her mouth. "So, when did you lose your virginity to His Royal Hotness?" she asked, her eyes gleaming with mischief.

"Excuse me?" Lara knew her mouth was open, but she couldn't seem to close it, any more than she could prevent the sudden, hard slamming of her heart within her chest. They couldn't possibly know! Nobody, aside from her parents and Val—and Graeme, of course— knew that she had relinquished her virginity to him five years earlier. In the years since, she'd been so careful not to let anyone find out....

The woman grinned as she observed the hot color that turned Lara's neck pink. "I mean, when did you first discover Graeme Hamilton? When did you first realize you were smitten?"

Just over five years ago, when I was almost eighteen years old and nobody in the entertainment industry even knew Graeme Hamilton existed.

She looked at the expectant faces of the women. How would they react if she told them the truth? If she told them that she had known Graeme before he became Hollywood's hottest heartthrob? That she knew him intimately? That she'd fallen in love with him the first time she'd met him and had lied to him about her age, telling him that she was actually twenty-one and not seventeen? He'd been twenty-three and she'd known instinctively that he wouldn't want anything to do with her if he realized just how young she was. Then, when their relationship had turned serious, she hadn't dared tell him the truth for fear of losing him. She'd continued the pretense of being a college student from California right up until after they'd eloped, when her father had tracked them down at the small Scottish inn where'd they'd spent their wedding night and dragged her from Graeme's bed, telling him in explicit terms just what he'd done with a minor.

What would these women think if she told them that particular story? That she'd spent two days and nights locked in a bedroom with Graeme? That she'd kissed, licked and nibbled every delicious part of his body?

They'd never believe her. They'd think she was making it up, and she wouldn't blame them. There were times when it didn't seem real to her. Sometimes, that long-ago summer seemed no more than a dream.

"I've been a fan of Graeme Hamilton's since before he made *Galaxy's End,*" she finally said. That, at least, was the truth.

"Well, welcome to the club," the first woman said. "My name is Sandra."

"And I'm Claire," the second woman added, indicating the registration badge she wore on a lanyard around her neck. "We're both from Wisconsin."

"I'm Lara. From Chicago."

At that moment the band stopped playing, and a spotlight was turned onto the stage next to where Lara and her companions were sitting. As they watched, a round woman dressed in a figure-hugging prison-guard costume stepped forward and took the microphone.

"Good evening, ladies and gentlemen," she said, in a Southern accent. "Welcome to the second annual *Galaxy's End* convention, where we joyfully celebrate everything related to that fabulous series, now in its third season." She waggled her eyebrows meaningfully. "And we especially want to celebrate the gorgeous actor who made us women long to be marooned on that uncharted planet."

There was scattered applause, and somebody from the back of the ballroom shouted, "We want Graeme!" followed by a ripple of laughter and more applause.

"I want to draw your attention to a slight change in our scheduled events," the woman continued. "In your brochure, you'll notice we have Finn McDougall, the director, scheduled to make a few remarks tonight. Unfortunately—"

She was interrupted by a collective groan of disappointment from the crowd, and she held her hands up, smiling.

"Now, let me finish, people. *Unfortunately*, Mr. McDougall's flight has been delayed and we've rescheduled his chat for tomorrow morning instead. However…" She smiled secretively at the crowd. "We didn't want you to be too disappointed, so we've brought in

another guest. Ladies and gentlemen, please welcome…
Mr. Graeme Hamilton!"

There was an instant of stunned silence before the
ballroom erupted in thunderous applause and ear-
splitting shrieks of approval. Then, from the wings of
the stage, a lean figure emerged, wearing Kip Corrigan's
signature black pants and shirt. The band struck up a
resounding rendition of the theme song from *Galaxy's
End,* and amidst the swell of music, the man did a
quick two-step dance move for the crowd, unleashing
another, louder round of applause and screaming, before
he strode across the stage toward the microphone.

Graeme saluted the band, kissed the emcee on both
cheeks and then turned to the crowd with a wave. The
spotlight turned his cropped hair into a gleaming halo
of brown and bronze highlights, and from where Lara
sat, a mere twenty feet from the stage, she could see his
easy grin and the way his blue-green eyes scanned the
crowd.

She couldn't move. Couldn't breathe.

For an instant, her heart stopped beating, and then it
exploded back into frenzied action. Lara had known
that when she finally saw Graeme again she'd have a
strong physical reaction, but never in her wildest imaginings had she thought she might actually expire on the
spot.

Graeme was speaking into the microphone, but Lara
couldn't hear anything beyond the roaring of her own
blood in her ears. From where she sat, she could see
the changes that five years had wrought, sculpting his
face, tracing it with experience, and turning it from
attractive to unforgettable. Lara felt something in her
chest tear free with a painful wrench. She was only

dimly aware of women rising from the nearby tables and moving forward, jostling each other in their urgency to get closer to the stage.

Closer to *him*.

Her mask was suffocating her.

She couldn't breathe, and fluttering wings of blackness appeared at the outer edges of her vision. She felt overheated and flushed. Suddenly, the small bottle of wine and two martinis she'd consumed threatened to make a reappearance.

She surged to her feet with a muttered apology, intent only on escaping the ballroom, unaware that the trailing edge of the tablecloth had become snagged on her metal bikini bottom. Lara turned to leave, dragging the tablecloth with her. As if in slow motion, plates of food and glassware crashed to the floor and the six costumed women who had been sitting with her scrambled to get out of the way, knocking over chairs and crying out in surprise.

For a moment, the band stopped playing and it seemed every face in the ballroom turned in her direction. Horrified, Lara looked toward the stage.

Graeme stared back at her.

For one, brief instant, their gazes collided. A renewed surge of heat swept through Lara, fierce and swift, and then receded, leaving her bathed in a cold, clammy sweat.

With a small sound of despair, she jerked the tablecloth free of her costume and fled toward the nearest exit, which opened into a service corridor. She was only dimly aware of the hotel staff passing on either side of her as she dashed toward an elevator at the end of the hallway. A startled waiter scooted out of her way as she flung herself at the doors, frantically pressing the button for them to open.

"Whoa, Princess Leia, that's a private service elevator," the waiter gasped, staring at her in dismay. "Jesus, what the hell is going on?"

Following his gaze, Lara glanced back in the direction she'd come from, and nearly fainted with panic. Graeme Hamilton himself was sprinting toward her, and hot on his heels was a horde of lust-crazed women, arms outstretched as they screamed his name.

Behind her, the elevator doors swished open and Lara flung herself inside. With her breath coming in painful hitches, she desperately punched at the buttons and watched with growing dread as Graeme and the pursuing crowd of women rapidly closed the distance between them.

"Please, please, please," she whispered, but whether her chant was for Graeme to reach the elevator in time, or not, she couldn't say.

Closer. Closer.

The doors started to swish shut, but even as Lara sagged against the wall in utter relief, a hand thrust itself between them, forcing them open. Lara watched in dismay as Graeme squeezed through, his breathing harsh. He pressed the button to close the doors and held his finger there, even as he took a protective stance in the opening. At the last instant, when it seemed the women would simply stampede him, the elevator doors closed.

"Christ," he muttered, and his voice washed over her, stirring her senses and catapulting her back five years.

Lara drank in the sight of him. He was larger than she

remembered. He completely dominated the small space, and she fisted her hands behind her back to keep from reaching out and touching him. She pressed herself into the corner of the compartment and hardly dared to breathe.

Maybe he wouldn't notice her.

Maybe, if she was very lucky, the elevator's dim lighting and the mask would be enough to keep him from recognizing her, although she knew the likelihood of that happening was about nil. How humiliating to be caught attending a fan festival for your ex-husband...current husband. Whatever.

With any luck, he wouldn't realize who she was, and he'd think she was merely playing out her role of submissive slave by keeping her head down. Her heart still thudded hard against her ribs and her palms were slick with moisture.

She'd wanted to see Graeme, but not like this, and especially not in a state of near undress! Everything about this first encounter was wrong. She'd wanted to be on solid footing, suitably garbed in her best business suit so that he'd have no doubts that she'd both grown up and moved on. She'd wanted to be self-assured and emotionally distant, not a pile of quivering nerve endings and heightened awareness.

He eased himself away from the doors and leaned negligently against the opposite wall. "That was a close one. Especially since the weight capacity on this lift canna exceed two thousand pounds."

His voice sank into her bones, heating her from the inside out. Slowly, Lara raised her gaze to his and felt the shock of it all the way to her toes. And just like the first time she'd seen him, everything else seemed to vanish.

She was no longer aware of being in a tiny elevator.

She didn't care that she wore next to nothing.

She was only aware of Graeme, and the sight of him, so incredibly sexy and masculine, caused her brain to misfire so that instead of saying something smart and sophisticated, the only thing that came out of her mouth was a stuttered, "Huh?"

He didn't smile, just continued to watch her intently. "I hate to be the one to break this to ye, princess," he murmured, his Scottish burr turning her insides to mush, "but the *Star Wars* convention isn't for another two months."

Distressed, Lara felt her stomach do a sick flip. Was it her imagination, or had he placed a subtle emphasis on the word *princess?* He'd always called her his princess; it had been his pet name for her back when they'd first met. Did he recognize her, or was it just her overactive imagination playing tricks on her?

She'd been so certain that he *had* recognized her, that he'd come barreling after her because he knew who she was and wanted retribution. She'd expected a bitter confrontation, but Graeme was looking at her without a trace of shock or anger or recrimination in his eyes.

In fact, if she wasn't mistaken, his expression was one of pure, male appreciation, and the heat in his eyes sparked an answering flame. The panic in her chest eased up a bit, and Lara didn't know whether to laugh or cry.

As impossible as it seemed, Graeme Hamilton didn't have a clue who she was.

Lara dragged her gaze away from his, her mind racing.

He didn't know it was her.

A part of her knew she should feel hurt that he didn't recognize her, but another part of her thrilled at the knowledge that he still found her attractive. She reminded herself she'd changed in five years, just as Valerie had said. She'd filled out in some places and slimmed down in others. Combined with the mask and costume, it was no wonder he didn't know who she was. The thought actually gave her a little courage, and her earlier embarrassment at being caught wearing such a flagrantly sexy outfit vanished. Seeing Graeme's eyes darken with desire was like an aphrodisiac. Warm, honeyed tendrils of pleasure snaked through her. She shifted her weight and a sharp burst of desire speared through her.

It seemed that some things never changed. Graeme still had the ability to arouse her with no more than a look. Two minutes ago, she'd been desperate to get away from him. Now, in close quarters with him, all she could think about was getting even closer.

She felt reckless.

Irresponsible.

Knowing that her identity was safe only amped up the naughty thoughts that were chasing themselves through her head. Less than an hour ago, she'd stood in front of her mirror and fantasized about how Graeme might react if he saw her in this getup. Now she wondered how he would react if she indicated she'd be willing to play the role of a true pleasure slave.

Tomorrow, she would don her safe, staid business suit, arm herself with her briefcase of legal documents and demand that he sign the divorce papers she had with her. She would wish him all the best in his career and his life, and then she would leave.

But for tonight, she would cater to her inner seductress, secure in the knowledge that nobody would ever find out, not even Graeme. She acknowledged that she wanted—no, she *needed*—to know if sex with Graeme was as good as she remembered, or if girlish memories had blown it out of proportion over the years. She had no illusions of trying to recapture the love of her youth; rather, she'd finally be able to put it firmly in her past and move on with her future. She'd been so young back then, so easily impressed. Not that she'd had much hands-on experience in the years since they'd been apart, but she'd done a lot of reading…and writing… about sex. In her fan fiction stories, Kip Corrigan was the ultimate lover, and most of what she wrote was based on her own experiences with Graeme during the two nights they'd shared.

But nobody could be *that* good, right?

3

RECOGNITION punched Graeme in the gut like a sledgehammer.

He'd thought about this moment more times than he cared to admit over the past five years, and in his mind their reunion had played out in all kinds of different ways. But his fantasies always ended the same way— with Lara in his bed, promising that she'd never leave again.

But now that she was here, he didn't have a fucking clue what to say. So he took a deep breath and turned to look at her, but was so completely blown away by the erotic vision she made that all he could manage was some ignorant remark about the weight capacity of the lift.

Because never, even in his most outrageous fantasies, could he have envisioned Lara looking like the woman who stared at him now from the opposite side of the elevator. For just a moment, his confidence faltered and he wondered if he might be mistaken. After all, he hadn't seen her in several years. Even in his most lurid and explicit imaginings, she looked perpetually the way she had that summer in London.

Sweet.

Shy.

Conservative.

For a moment, his chest clenched hard and tight, and his hands fisted at his sides in recalled frustration. He'd been a struggling actor, just out of drama school, trying desperately to make a name for himself in the London theater scene where actors were ten a penny. His strong Scots accent and his strapping, blue-collar physique had worked against him, however, and the best he'd been able to manage had been amateur productions in second-rate theaters.

He'd been performing in a stage presentation of *Blood Brothers,* in front of a nearly empty theater, when *she* had walked in and sat in the back row. She'd come back every day until the last performance, when she'd chosen to sit in the front row.

After the show had ended, he'd sprinted out of the theater to intercept her, because meeting her had been a compulsion he couldn't resist. He'd realized there was something special about her even though back then, she'd looked more like a modern-day Sandra Dee with her buttoned-up blouses, her little designer handbags and ridiculous shoes. But in less than a week of meeting her for afternoon tea, taking walks along the Thames and exploring the city together, he'd fallen completely and irrevocably in love. He'd never understood what it was that she'd seen in him, but he did know one thing; he wanted her more than he'd ever wanted another girl in his life.

His mistake had been to believe the lies that had fallen so easily from those cherub lips; that she was a twenty-one-year-old college student spending a summer abroad. That she only had one year of college left. That she was legally old enough to get married.

That she loved him.

Now he could hardly comprehend that his young wife and this exotic creature might be one and the same. He'd barely stepped onto the stage back in the ballroom, when a woman at a nearby table had suddenly lurched to her feet and done a bad rendition of the old tablecloth trick, dumping every place setting onto the floor in a cacophony of shattered dishware.

She'd been dressed in an eye-popping Princess Leia slave-girl costume that left absolutely nothing to the imagination. Graeme had paused, prepared to make a joke about escapees from Jabba the Hutt's harem, when he'd found himself looking past the gold mask and straight into a pair of eyes that he'd recognize anywhere.

Shock had slammed through him, but she was gone before he could react, pushing past the crowd and vanishing through a side door. Graeme hadn't paused to think about his actions. He'd leaped from the stage, intent only upon catching the woman. But the mob of costumed fans had other ideas and for several frustrating seconds, he'd found himself sinking beneath a surging mass of greedy females who'd clamored for an autograph, a photo, a hug, a kiss. He might never have escaped their clutches if it hadn't been for his publicist and hotel security, pushing their way through the crowd and extricating him from the surging mass of women.

With muttered apologies, he'd broken free and dashed through the side door, his eyes searching the area beyond. He was rewarded when he saw Princess Leia frantically trying to access a service elevator. With a low growl, he'd plunged down the corridor after her, only dimly aware of the shrieking women who'd pursued him.

As he'd sprinted down the hallway, he knew his gut had been right; the woman was Lara. A glossy braid swung between her shoulder blades, the color of a brand-new penny. In five years, he'd never come across another person with hair that unique shade of copper, and despite the fact her body had definitely changed— in a bite-your-fist, hold-me-back kind of way—there was absolutely no question in his mind that the woman trying so desperately to escape was her.

He'd had an instant of panic when she bolted into the elevator and the doors began to close, but a burst of adrenaline had propelled him forward enough that he got his hand inside. He'd thrust himself through the doors and into the compartment with her.

For a split second, he'd registered the utter dismay in her sapphire eyes, before he'd abruptly turned his back on her. Aside from preventing the hordes of fans from mobbing the elevator, he'd needed to get a grip on himself.

As impossible as it seemed, Lara was *here*. And clearly, not too pleased that he'd followed her.

Graeme didn't know what kind of reaction he'd expected, but it sure as hell hadn't been *this*. She was simply staring at him from behind the ornate mask as if she didn't know him from Adam. As if she hadn't just fled the ballroom with him in hot pursuit. As if she hadn't noticed the pack of screaming women who'd been hot on his heels.

As if he hadn't—once upon a time—explored every luscious inch of her body with his hands and mouth.

There was no greeting, no how-do-you-do, no nothing. Instead, she gave him a polite, distant little smile and let her gaze drift away from him, fixing her attention on the blinking numbers over the door as if she had no freaking idea who he was.

As if they were complete strangers.

Which was nuts, because even if she didn't recognize him as the man she'd once *married,* he was still Graeme Hamilton. If his publicist was to be believed, every woman who'd registered for the convention had done so because she was a huge Graeme Hamilton fan.

Then it hit him.

Lara was hoping like hell that he wouldn't recognize her. She didn't *want* him to recognize her. Graeme knew the body language well enough, since he frequently employed the same tactic when he left his Los Angeles apartment.

But did she really think he wouldn't know who she was? That a mask would be enough to throw him? He'd recognize her anywhere. Even now, her scent was driving him insane, the same way it had done five years ago. It was an intoxicating blend of something light and exotic that was hers alone. He could pick her out of a crowd even if he was blindfolded.

Shit. He needed a drink. But he'd learned the hard way that drinking wouldn't help him forget Lara, no matter how desperate he might be.

Memories shoved their way inside his mind and he could still see her spread out beneath him. Lara, her red-gold hair splayed out across the crisp linens. Her lush lips parted, sapphire eyes glazed with pleasure. Her back arched, and her pale breasts thrusting upward, their rosy nipples tempting him. Her limbs wrapped around him, her heat gripping him, drawing him in as she urged him to thrust faster, deeper—

Shit. *Shit.*

What the hell game was she playing at? There was only one reason he could think of for her being here; she wanted out of their marriage. Memories of the two nights they'd spent together still caused his toes to curl with recalled lust. But despite what he and Lara had shared—and they'd shared plenty—she'd walked out of his life forty-eight hours after their wedding.

But the nightmare hadn't ended there. The day after Lara left, when Graeme had returned to his tiny apartment in London, Brent Whitfield had paid him a visit, accompanied by a lawyer and two government agents.

Graeme had been shocked by the news that her father was the U.S. Ambassador to England. Brent Whitfield came from a long and prominent line of political servants, and if his influential lineage wasn't enough to make Graeme feel like a peasant, the Whitfield family money would have. But Graeme had never believed that money made one person better than another. While he could appreciate that Brent wanted to protect his daughter from avaricious money-grubbers, the way he'd treated Graeme had been unforgivable.

Graeme still saw red when he recalled the accusations that Lara's father had hurled at him. He'd made Graeme feel like the worst kind of low-life scum, as though he was morally corrupt. He'd threatened to have Graeme arrested for statutory rape, but Graeme had known just enough about Scottish law to know that his marriage to Lara had been legitimate and would hold up in court.

Refusing to sign those annulment papers had given him a fierce sense of satisfaction. He'd made a promise to Lara's father that day; if Lara wanted out of the marriage, she'd have to tell him so to his face. He'd have no problem letting her go; all she needed to do was ask him herself. But she hadn't had the guts to.

There had been a couple of times over the past five years when he'd almost filed the papers himself so that he could move on with his life, but both times he'd chickened out.

She'd been in college—for real, this time—and he hadn't wanted to disrupt her studies. And if he was honest with himself, part of the reason he hadn't pushed the divorce was because so long as she was married to him, she couldn't get too serious about anyone else.

Now here she was, looking like something out of his freaking dreams, but he knew the reason for her sudden reappearance in his life had nothing to do with making his fantasies come true. She wanted a divorce, probably to marry the guy she was rumored to be romantically involved with.

It had been ridiculously easy for Graeme to keep tabs on her activities over the years. With social networking Web sites like Facebook and MySpace, combined with her prominent family name, he'd had no trouble finding information about her. Or her theater program. Or the fact that she'd been dating one of her coworkers at the theater.

The thought of Lara with another man made his stomach tighten and his chest constrict. He'd known that eventually she'd seek him out and demand a divorce; a woman like Lara wasn't meant to live alone. She'd want to remarry, to have children. He just wasn't prepared for how that made him feel.

Graeme reminded himself yet again that he was over her. Hell, he'd already planned on ending their farce of a marriage soon. He'd decided he didn't want to risk the paparazzi unearthing the news; they'd have a field day with it, and Lara would suffer the most.

He'd also been offered a movie that would take him to New Zealand for the next eighteen months for filming. The deal symbolized a major shift in his career, from television to the big screen. Graeme hoped the move would also mark a major shift in his personal life, as well.

He needed to get out of Hollywood, away from the photographers and half-assed reporters who recorded his every move. Every day, he'd pick up a paper and read some bullshit story about his alleged affairs or his supposed addiction to drugs or alcohol. He couldn't so much as go for a morning jog without the paparazzi accosting him. Even stopping somewhere for a quick bite to eat had become more trouble than it was worth, with women following him down the street, giggling and shouting obscene suggestions, and doing anything they could to attract his attention.

Leeches, all of them.

Only Lara, standing on the other side of the elevator and acting as if he didn't exist, seemed unimpressed by either him or his fame.

He looked at her, but she pointedly ignored him. Well, fine. Two could play at her game. If she wanted to be incognito, far be it from him to destroy the illusion. There was a reason he was one of Hollywood's top actors; he could pretend with the best of them.

He gave her a languid smile and dropped his voice an octave. "I hate to be the one to break this to ye, princess, but the *Star Wars* convention isn't for another two months."

She turned slowly in his direction, as if she was uncertain whether he was speaking to her. Her eyes
widened behind the gold mask. For just a second,
Graeme was sure she was going to fold, that she'd ac-
knowledge him, pull the mask away from her face and
finally, after five goddamned long years, they'd talk
about what had happened between them.

Instead, she studied him from behind the mask, nibbling on her plump lower lip. He knew the instant she
decided to continue the charade. As he watched, her
entire body posture changed and softened. She leaned
one shoulder against the wall and tipped her head to the
side as she considered him. Her sapphire eyes traveled
over every inch of him, as if measuring his worth.
Graeme had to force himself to remain relaxed and
keep his expression one of amused interest, while his
blood thudded hard through his veins and a combination of dread and anticipation coiled in his stomach.

"Maybe I'm not looking for the *Star Wars* convention," she finally said. Her voice was breathless, but
Graeme didn't miss how she surreptitiously swiped her
palms over the scarlet fabric that covered her rear.
Another man might have interpreted the move as sexual,
designed to thrust those amazing breasts forward, but he
guessed she was nervous and that her hands were damp
with perspiration. The thought gave him a little courage.

"So then, what *are* ye looking for?"

"Maybe I'm looking for a man to…master me." Her
voice was laced with naughty suggestion, and Graeme's
body responded instantly to the implicit promise in
her tone, even as his brain tried to comprehend that
Lara—his sweet, innocent Lara—was actually proposi-
tioning him.

He devoured her with his eyes, noting every detail about her. The passing years had been more than generous to her. She was the same, yet different. Gone was the self-conscious, conservative girl he'd known. In her place was a curvy woman whose lush body completely blew him away.

Five years ago, her breasts would have fitted neatly into the palms of his hands; now they threatened to spill out of the insubstantial top. The creamy skin that swelled above the gold-embossed cups mesmerized him, made him want to pull the top down and explore the perfect, rosy tips he knew were hidden beneath. Her waist was narrow, and his gaze devoured the feminine curve of her belly above the metal bikini.

He had an almost overwhelming urge to drop to his knees and press his mouth against the delicate whorl of her navel. His palms ached to stroke and cup the smooth flesh of her buttocks, only partially hidden by the flimsy drape of crimson fabric.

Somewhere, alarm bells went off. He ignored them, acknowledging wryly that he'd never been able to think logically where Lara was concerned. Whenever he was near her, he stopped thinking about anything except touching her, kissing her and being inside her. She had an innate sweetness that even the blatantly sexy costume couldn't conceal. He found the combination irresistible.

Knowing he was playing a dangerous game, he reached out and hit the stop button on the elevator, and they slid smoothly to a halt somewhere between the thirty-first and thirty-second floors. Lara's eyes flared briefly, but she didn't protest.

Graeme stepped forward until he crowded her

against the far wall. Inwardly, his heart rate accelerated, and it took all his self-restraint not to shake her and demand to know what game she was playing. Outwardly, he kept his composure. He let his gaze slip down over her masked face and settle on her lips.

Her mouth had always distracted him. Slightly fuller on the top, her lips had a puffy, just-been-kissed fullness that made him visualize all the hedonistic things she could do with them besides talk, especially when she moistened them with the pink tip of her tongue.

He braced his hands on either side of her head, effectively trapping her, and inhaled her fragrance. Her own breathing was quick and shallow, and for one crazy second, Graeme thought he could actually smell her desire. It went straight to his head, making him ditch whatever good intentions he might have had.

"Sounds tempting," he finally murmured, his breath close enough to stir the wisps of hair at her temple. "Although, I should warn you, it's been a long time since I've met a woman who could fulfill my every desire."

He was vaguely aware that his Scottish accent had become more pronounced, the way it always did when he become agitated—or aroused. Did she guess that he referred to her and their long-ago wedding night?

Then she touched him, and he ceased to think. As touches went, it wasn't much, but as she trailed the tip of one slender finger down the length of his arm, he could have sworn the contact scorched him through the fabric of his sleeve.

She glanced at him through lowered lashes. "Now why does that sound like a challenge?"

Her finger drifted from his arm to his chest, where it wandered in a seemingly random path and followed the shallow groove between his pectorals. He closed his eyes briefly against the exquisite sensation. Lara's sultry tone completed the erotic fantasy, weaving its way through his head. It would be so easy to do this, to lose himself in her and pretend the past five years had never happened, pretend that she was still his.

He thought he'd done a pretty good job of burying the memories of their brief relationship. After she'd left him, he'd gone through a dark period where he hadn't exactly been celibate. He'd had his share of women. Beautiful women. They'd looked good on his arm, and they'd been more than happy to spend time with him, doing whatever it was he wanted them to do. But none of them had tempted or aroused him the way Lara did now, with her cherub lips and her soft, lush curves.

He swallowed hard.

"Is that what I am to you?" he asked softly. "A challenge?"

She smiled, a secretive smile that should have had him punching the elevator buttons in a desperate bid for escape. Instead, he dipped his head to catch her words.

"Oh, yes. You might just be my greatest challenge ever." Then she stood on her toes and pressed that soft, moist mouth against the corner of his, and he was a goner.

Graeme groaned, knowing he was so screwed. He couldn't do this…couldn't let her pull him back into the sweet, forbidden pleasure of her arms, even for a single night.

But as her fingers slid to the back of his neck and

urged his head down, he acknowledged ruefully that some things never changed. He still had no ability to resist her. He'd give her anything she wanted, and right now it seemed she wanted *him*.

4

LARA DIDN'T KNOW what had gotten into her, only that when Graeme didn't recognize her, something inside her had loosened and then let go completely. She'd come to Las Vegas to exorcise her demons, she just hadn't expected to do so in quite this way. But she understood now that the only way to let Graeme go was to get him out of her system once and for all.

She'd spent the past few years writing explicit stories about the character he played in *Galaxy's End,* and her vivid descriptions of Kip's sexual prowess had ranged from tender and considerate to fiercely demanding and masterful. But whatever the situation, he always left the heroine sated and weak with pleasure. Lara didn't doubt that Graeme knew how to please a woman, but she doubted that he was as good as the fictional character he portrayed.

She'd been living in a fantasy world of her own making for way too long. Tonight, she'd get a healthy dose of reality. The challenge would be to keep her head firmly in the present and not pretend that he was still in love with her.

This wasn't about love.

If there had ever been any love involved, it had died the day her father had discovered them together in the little inn in Scotland and told Graeme the truth about how she had tricked him into marrying her.

From the moment he'd thrust his big body into the elevator with her, she'd realized that five years had done nothing to diminish her desire for him, and wearing the costume somehow fueled that need. The outfit made her feel sexy and bold in a way she'd never experienced before. Even on their wedding night, when she'd done things she'd only ever fantasized about, she hadn't been completely uninhibited. She'd wanted to please Graeme, but her actions had been tempered to a certain degree by her own self-consciousness.

Disguised as Princess Leia, however, she felt both powerful and irresistible, as if she could do anything. Even seduce Graeme Hamilton. Maybe the alcohol she'd consumed had gone to her head, because she felt incredibly sexy, like the kind of women Graeme escorted to his world premieres, the kind of women he probably slept with.

She pushed down the niggling sense of hurt that he didn't recognize her, reminding herself that five years had passed since he'd last seen her. She'd changed during that time. Besides, the gold mask concealed most of her face, and he probably hadn't given her more than a passing thought in recent years, if he'd thought of her at all. She should be grateful for the disguise because if he realized just who she was, he'd want nothing to do with her.

Now here she was, stopped in an elevator with the sexiest man alive, contemplating things that had nothing to do with getting his autograph. The entire scenario might have come directly from one of her own erotic stories. His heated words coursed through her like a challenge…*it's been a long time since I've met a woman who could fulfill my every desire.*

For tonight at least, Lara intended to fulfill every one of his desires, and a few of her own, too.

His skin was hot beneath her fingers as she urged his head down, and she thought he gave a small groan as she brushed her lips across his. For just an instant he resisted, his body stiff and unresponsive against hers, before he dragged in a shuddering breath and slanted his mouth hard across Lara's.

The heat of his kiss took her breath away. She hadn't forgotten the potency of Graeme's kisses, but her reaction to them was almost a physical pain. Every cell in her body leaped at his touch and strained forward, yearning for more. Her blood warmed and then slid through her heated veins until her entire body simmered.

Reaching up, he captured her hands in his and then pinned them against the wall behind her head, using the weight of his body to hold her in place. His lips were hot and hungry as they moved over hers, coaxing and enticing a response. Lara whimpered softly and her lips parted of their own volition. Graeme's tongue teased her, stroking and exploring the recesses of her mouth until her head spun. A warm, sweet fullness slowly blossomed in her belly, spreading outward until her breasts tingled and ached for his touch, and her legs felt they would no longer support her.

She was barely aware when he released her hands and slid his down the bare skin of her back, his fingers smoothing along her spine until he reached the top edge of the bikini bottom. Her own hands moved to his shoulders as he pulled her more fully against him, the muscles in his arms bunching under her fingers.

He groaned softly against her mouth and his lips changed, became more urgent, possessing her completely as his hand spread downward over the curve of her hip and captured one buttock, pressing her intimately against his body so that she was suddenly, vividly aware of the rigid length of his arousal pressing against her belly.

The knowledge that she could still arouse him made her senses soar. She wouldn't think about the fact that he didn't know who she was and that he was only responding to her physically, that it was just sex. Right now, sex with Graeme Hamilton sounded perfect. She wouldn't think about tomorrow, and she definitely wouldn't think about Christopher.

As kind and sweet as Christopher was, he'd never made her want to peel her clothes off and feel the hot glide of his skin against hers. They'd come close to having sex on a couple of different occasions, but she'd backed off at the last minute, though she'd been unable to explain why.

Now she understood.

Because as much as she liked Christopher, he'd never made her feel that she might spontaneously combust if she couldn't have him inside her, stroking her to a frenzied pitch while he whispered heated words against her flesh.

Dragging her mouth from Graeme's, she trailed her lips across his skin to his ear, swirling her tongue around the edge before taking his lobe between her teeth and biting gently, gratified when she heard his hissing intake of breath.

"Let's go to my room," she whispered, punctuating her words with a soft bite to his jaw, before soothing the area with her tongue. "I can't wait much longer."

"My room is closer," he rasped, and withdrew a card from his back pocket.

Still holding her firmly against him, he reached out and slid the key card into a slot above the buttons, and then punched the fortieth floor. The elevator glided briefly upward and stopped. Graeme pulled her into a small lobby that was lavishly decorated with marble and crystal, and Lara saw a security guard at the far end, near a second elevator. She knew without having to be told that this must be the penthouse suite, the luxurious rooms reserved only for the very important or the very wealthy.

"Good evening, Mr. Hamilton," the guard greeted them. His face was carefully impassive, but Lara could hear the surprise in his voice. "I wasn't expecting you to come up on the service elevator."

"Yes, well, things got a little out of hand at the masquerade ball," he said tersely, leading Lara toward a hotel-room door. "I'm not expecting any visitors tonight, so…" He let his voice trail off meaningfully, and the security guard inclined his head.

"I understand. Nobody will disturb you. Have a good evening, Mr. Hamilton."

"Thanks." At that moment, Graeme's cell phone buzzed at his hip, discordant and insistent. Graeme paused outside the door to his suite and with a meaningful look at Lara, opened the phone. Even from where she stood, Lara could hear the loud, strident voice on the other end, demanding to know where Graeme was, and telling him that he needed to come back down to the ballroom. Graeme closed his eyes briefly and a flicker of annoyance crossed his face.

"Forget it, Tony," he finally bit out. "I'm not coming

back down there. I don't care what you tell them, but I'm done for the night." Without waiting for a reply, he snapped his cell phone closed and then turned the power off.

"My publicist," he muttered, in way of explanation. "I'm sorry for the interruption."

His tone was so rueful that Lara felt a pang of sympathy for him. She couldn't imagine what it must be like, to have your schedule dictated by the demands of a greedy public.

Graeme opened the door and pushed Lara through before closing it firmly behind them. She had a brief impression of an elegant, spacious apartment with floor-to-ceiling windows overlooking the Las Vegas strip, before Graeme pushed her up against the wall and completely enfolded her in his arms. His hands were everywhere, sliding over her bare skin, skimming over her hips and cupping and kneading her buttocks beneath the metal of the bikini bottom.

"Christ," he muttered, and he buried his face in her neck, pressing his lips against her throat. "You're so beautiful. I have to see all of you."

As if to prove his point, he hooked his thumbs inside the top of her bikini and tugged it downward, until her breasts popped free. For a moment, he just looked, and Lara was too enthralled by the expression in his eyes to feel shocked or self-conscious at the unexpected exposure. Then there was no more room for thought as he cupped her breasts almost reverently, his big hands closing over them, rubbing the nipples with his thumbs until they stood out, stiff and rosy.

"I need to taste you," he muttered, and bent his head to lave one distended tip with his tongue.

If not for the fact that her body was pressed between Graeme's hard warmth and the wall, Lara might have collapsed from the sheer pleasure that knifed through her. The sight of Graeme's dark head against her naked breasts was like an erotic elixir, and she couldn't stop her hands from burying themselves in his hair, feeling the heat from his scalp warm her fingers as she laced them through the short strands.

He was cupping her breasts, lifting them and kneading them as he suckled her. His mouth was hot and wet, and when he rolled one nipple gently between his teeth, lust speared through Lara's midsection and swamped her with moisture.

Somewhere in the functioning part of her brain, she was aware of the heated urgency in Graeme's lovemaking, and the rawness of it both shocked and thrilled her. Five years ago, he'd been the perfect lover, intent only upon her pleasure even if it meant tamping down his own desire. Only after she'd assured him she wasn't as fragile as he believed had he dropped some of his self-restraint and loved her with a potent force that had stolen her breath.

Right now, he exhibited all of the force and none of the restraint as he lavished attention on her breasts. When he finally lifted his head, it was to capture her lips in a kiss that dragged her very soul from her depths, plundering her mouth as his hands traveled over her body, stroking and caressing her bare skin.

With supreme effort, Lara twisted her face away. Her heart slammed in her chest. Her head felt fuzzy, as if she'd had too much to drink, and she had the distinct sensation that if it weren't for the weight of Graeme's body holding her firmly against the wall, she'd float away.

"Wait," she finally gasped, pushing at his wide shoulders until he moved fractionally away from her, although his hands still roamed across the bare skin of her back. "This is supposed to be about your pleasure—about me pleasuring you."

"Oh, you do, love," he rumbled softly. "You do."

Lara laughed unsteadily. "I'm glad you approve, but I really want to do this my way."

Graeme blew out a hard breath and bent his head to hers. "If you really want to pleasure me, you'll take this damned mask off and let me see your face properly."

Panic churned through Lara's stomach as her brain worked furiously to come up with a plausible argument for keeping the mask in place. "No, I don't think I will," she finally said, but softened her words with a soft sweep of her mouth over his. "For tonight, the mask stays on. I think it adds a bit of…mystery, don't you? Trust me, you won't mind a bit."

There was a momentary silence, and then he shrugged. "Okay, fine. Right now, you can do whatever the hell you want and you won't hear a whisper of complaint from me."

"That's what I hoped you'd say," Lara replied, distracted by how his eyes glittered with desire, more green now than blue. "I have a few things in mind that I'm pretty sure you won't complain about."

Lara's fingers went to the buttons of his black shirt, and popped the first one from its hole.

"First," she murmured, hoping he didn't see the faint tremor in her hands as she worked her way to the second button and released it, "I'm going to unbutton your shirt and kiss every inch of skin that I see."

To prove her words, she separated the fabric and

dropped a moist kiss to the bronzed skin she exposed, touching him with the tip of her tongue. He didn't make a sound, just watched her face with an expression of absorption.

She moved to the third button, and then the fourth, aware her pulse had begun to accelerate as her fingers descended toward his belt. With each button that she freed, she pushed the shirt away and pressed her lips and tongue against his flesh, following the light furring of chest hair that narrowed as it reached his navel, and then disappeared beneath the waistband of his trousers.

Despite the fact she wore next to nothing, she was hot. Feverish. By the time she popped the last button free, she was crouching in front of him. He loomed over her, with his hands braced on the wall above her, staring intently down at her. Her position was one of feminine supplication, not at all unlike a slave girl pleasuring her master. Her bare breasts, pushed upward by the bunched fabric of the bikini top, made her feel wanton, especially when his gaze devoured her.

Swallowing hard, Lara tugged his shirttails free and leaned forward to press her mouth against his stomach, just below his navel. His muscles contracted at the intimate contact. Emboldened, Lara touched her tongue lightly to the spot, and then traced a circle around his belly button. He gave a soft murmur of encouragement, and she hooked her fingers into his belt loops as she worked her way back up his torso.

His stomach was layered in muscle. Lara ran her tongue along the shallow groove that bisected his chest, only vaguely aware that his breathing seemed labored. When she reached his pectorals, she glanced up at him. His eyes were slumberous now, watching her with a seductive intensity that caused her body temperature to rise and liquid heat to pool at her center.

Tentatively, half expecting him to protest, Lara skated her lips over his heated flesh and flicked at the small nub of one nipple with her tongue. He made a guttural sound in his throat and Lara lapped the small bud before taking it into her mouth the way he had done with her just minutes before. He stiffened, but made no move to pull away.

With her tongue still tormenting him, she pushed impatiently at the fabric of his shirt. "Take this off," she breathed against his skin. "I want to see you."

Graeme straightened and shrugged the shirt from his shoulders, letting it slide along the length of his arms until it fell onto the floor behind him. Resting back on her heels, with her fingers still holding his belt loops, Lara looked up at him and all the breath in her lungs whooshed out.

His shoulders and arms were powerful and bunched with muscles. His chest was a slab of granite, with a sculpted six-pack that was so defined she could have lost her loose change in the grooves.

Five years ago, he'd been lean and athletic. Now he was Herculean. Reaching down, he grasped her by the upper arms and hauled her to her feet.

"Whatever it is you have in mind," he rasped, "won't be done here, against the door. I'm not a complete barbarian."

"Oh, that's too bad," Lara murmured, but let herself be pulled upward. She leaned into him, allowing her bare breasts to press against his chest. "Where, then?"

She could sense his impatience, but wasn't prepared when he scooped her fully into his arms. With a small gasp, she flung her arms around his neck, but couldn't deny that she enjoyed the sensation of being weightless, as if lifting her caused him absolutely no strain whatsoever.

"Here," he said, striding into a bedroom that adjoined the living area of the suite. "Much better for what I have in mind."

He set her down on her feet next to the biggest bed Lara had ever seen in her life. Sumptuous swaths of champagne-colored silk cascaded from the ceiling and draped along either side of the headboard, and the bed itself was covered in a rich damask coverlet and heaped with pillows.

A small light burned on the bedside table, and Lara was only dimly aware of the discreet opulence that surrounded them, of the rich cream-and-beige color scheme, the paneled walls and the Louis XVI furnishings. Lara wasn't unaccustomed to lavish surroundings, but it had been many years since she'd been surrounded by such luxury, and it was a far cry from the tiny apartment where Graeme had lived when she first met him.

"You certainly know how to live," she commented, her eyes absorbing the details of the penthouse suite.

"I was given this room for security reasons." Graeme frowned. "Personally, I don't much care what my rooms look like, as long as they're clean."

"I'm not criticizing," Lara assured him softly. "The room is beautiful."

And in the middle of it all stood Graeme, looking every inch the masterful lord with his black pants and acres of bare, tanned skin. Lara could almost believe he was a sheikh or a sultan, entertaining a visit from his favorite harem girl in his private quarters.

And right now, *she* was that harem girl. His entire body was tightly coiled, anticipating the intense pleasure she would soon provide. Lara held on to the image she'd created in her head, finding it gave her courage. The mental picture she drew was at once so seductive and so intriguing, that she couldn't wait to make it a reality.

"You forget," she said, lowering her voice to a sultry tone as she slid her palms over the rise of his chest muscles, "this isn't about what you have in mind. I'm the one providing the pleasure and right now—" she paused to drop a soft, wet kiss against his throat "—it pleases me to kiss you. Everywhere." She punctuated her words with more wet kisses along his torso. "I want to taste you…to feel you beneath my mouth."

Graeme stood passively as she spoke, allowing her to press her mouth against his body, but when she sat down on the edge of the bed and drew him between her knees, he caught her braid in one hand, wrapping it around his fist as he tipped her head back and studied her masked face in the indistinct light.

"Why are you doing this?" he asked, his voice no more than a husky growl.

For an instant, Lara panicked, wondering if he'd guessed her identity, before she determinedly pushed her doubts aside. There was no way he could know who she was. If he did, he'd never have allowed her into his suite. As far as he knew, she was just an enthusiastic and eager fan.

"Why wouldn't I?" she countered, smoothing her hands along his rib cage. His skin was like hot silk beneath her fingers. "You're an incredibly gorgeous man. A woman would give a lot to be with a guy like you."

"Christ." He made a sound that was half laugh, half groan, before bending down and slanting his mouth hard across hers.

Clearly, he was through with talking, which suited Lara just fine, because she could think of so many things she'd rather do with her mouth.

Dragging her lips from his she concentrated instead on his hard-ridged stomach, stroking her lips along the flesh that rode just above his waistband, while her fingers worked his belt. His big hands descended to her shoulders and slid warmly along the length of her arms. When the button of his pants refused to cooperate beneath her trembling fingers, he swept them aside.

"Let me."

She watched in utter fascination as he popped the button free, and an eternity seemed to pass as he eased the zipper down, exposing the waistband of the cotton boxer shorts he wore beneath.

"Oh," Lara breathed, when she saw the hard thrust of his arousal beneath the material.

Pushing his pants down over his hips, she cupped him lightly through the boxers. He was hard and hot beneath the thin fabric. Lara slid her fingers beneath the stretchy waistband and eased the boxers down until his penis sprang free. Immediately, all the saliva in her mouth evaporated.

He was long and thick, and the head of his gorgeous erection strained toward her. How was it possible that she had forgotten how breathtaking the man was?

Slowly, as if mesmerized, Lara slid a finger along his length. "I want to do this, but with my tongue," she breathed.

Above her, she heard his breath hitch. His hands

cupped her face and his fingers began a slow, sensuous massage of the sensitive skin behind her ears. Slowly, Lara bent her head to him, sweeping his length with one long, wet pass of her tongue.

Graeme groaned loudly.

He tasted incredible. Intoxicating.

Her hands slid over him, letting instinct guide her as she as she took him fully into her mouth, her senses flooded with his taste and texture. She wanted to devour him, to lick and nibble and suck him until he cried out and his legs buckled beneath him. Instead, she took her time, wrapping her lips around his shaft and pulling softly on him, until he popped free of her mouth and she could run her tongue along the corona and tease the tiny slit at the top.

With her free hand, she stroked him from below, running her palm over his strong thighs and urging them apart so that she could cup and fondle his sac, and explore the smooth stretch of skin just behind. When she felt him tighten in her palm, she licked him like a lollipop, and then sucked on his length until he swelled even more.

With a guttural sound of intense pleasure, Graeme arched his hips toward her. She nearly groaned herself when he slid his hands down over her shoulders and cupped her naked breasts, his fingers teasing and plucking at the taut peaks until Lara couldn't think straight. Her body pulsed with need, weeping with moisture, her nerve endings so sensitized that she was in danger of having a spontaneous orgasm.

As if reading her thoughts, Graeme caught her face in his hands and forced her away. She released him reluctantly, but couldn't prevent her hands from continuing to stroke him.

"Stop," he ground out, "or I'm not going to last."

His breathing was fast and harsh, his expression pained, and she couldn't resist stroking her finger one last time across the top of his erection. It came away wet and glistening with proof of his arousal, and Lara deliberately put her finger in her mouth, sucking on the digit the way she had just suckled him. She slanted him what she hoped was a provocative look.

"Mmm," she hummed approvingly. "That was…delicious. I trust my master is pleased so far?"

5

GRAEME'S MOUTH went dry as he watched Lara suck her finger clean of his essence. His entire body throbbed with need, and he wanted nothing more than to push her back onto the wide bed and thrust himself into her welcoming heat. His cock twitched at the thought, and he didn't think he'd ever been as hard as he was now.

She was too hot.

Too tempting.

He was on fire, and the sight of her half-naked and on his bed was almost more than his poor, lust-sodden brain could handle. Every cell in his body cried out for her. She was all curves and sweet, satiny skin and he could willingly and easily lose himself in the pleasure her body promised. But the small part of his gray matter that still functioned demanded to know the reason for her sudden reappearance in his life, dressed as a slave girl who, apparently, couldn't wait to get her hands— or any other part of her delectable anatomy—around him.

His first thought had been that she'd finally come to demand an end to their marriage, and the strength of his emotions had shocked him. There had been denial, fierce and swift. Even after five years, he thought of

Lara as his. But he'd also been relieved to have the waiting finally come to an end.

He realized that a part of him had been living life on hold, anticipating that moment when Lara would reappear in his life and finally tell him that she wanted out.

Now here she was, and although it sure as hell seemed like a divorce was the last thing on her mind, Graeme had already made the decision to let her go. He'd thought he'd feel an enormous weight lift from his shoulders; he'd finally be free in every sense of the word.

Instead, he felt inexplicably angry and sad. Angry that she'd screwed things up so badly for them all those years ago, and sad that the resulting damage had been beyond repair. He'd been so furious with her for lying to him, and even more furious with her father for threatening to have him arrested. As if he was a criminal—nothing more than an ignorant thug with no breeding and no education.

But it had taken less than a week for his anger to subside. When he'd been able to think rationally, he'd understood that Lara must have loved him very much if she'd been willing to lie to him about her age and risk her father's anger by marrying him. Once his temper had cooled, he realized what a fool he'd been to let her go. He should have stood up to her father and taken Lara on any terms. He couldn't sleep, couldn't concentrate on anything except what he'd lost.

So he'd sold everything he'd had, borrowed a little more money from his mother, and purchased a one-way ticket to New York. He'd had it all worked out; Lara would attend Columbia University as her father had wanted. Graeme would get an apartment nearby and find work as an actor. He'd graduated from the Royal Academy of Dramatic Arts and he had some connections on Broadway. He didn't expect to land any major roles, just enough to ensure he had a steady income.

But when he'd reached New York, the customs officials told him that his visa had been denied for reasons related to "suspicion of criminal activity." He'd been stunned. His protests had been ignored. He'd been told he was not welcome in the United States, and he'd been put on a return flight to England. At the time, Graeme had wanted to howl with frustration and fury. There was only one person with the political clout and the personal motivation to keep him out of the country, and that was Brent Whitfield.

Graeme had returned to London with nothing; no job, no apartment and no hope of being reunited with Lara. His life had taken a downward spiral. Even now, with all his hard-earned success, he couldn't think of that time without his mood turning black.

Graeme pushed the thoughts aside and concentrated instead on the vision Lara made as she sat on the edge of his bed, watching him expectantly. In answer to her naughty question, he shucked his shoes and socks and shoved his pants down until he could kick them free. He saw Lara's eyes turn cobalt behind her mask and was glad for the grueling exercise regimen he followed that kept his body in top shape. Ignoring her cry of surprise, he hefted her into middle of the bed and followed her, pressing the length of his body against her own.

"Oh, yeah," he finally said, bending his head to one dusky nipple, "your…master…is more than pleased."

He flicked the hard tip with his tongue as he smoothed a hand over her stomach until he encountered the metal bikini bottom. "How the hell does this thing come off?"

Lara twisted toward him. "Here," she said breathlessly, indicating the metal loops at her hip. "They twist apart."

While he bent his attention to the mechanism, Lara did her best to distract him. She slid a leg over his and pressed her center against his erection. Her hands gripped his bottom, urging him closer. In all the years that they'd been apart, Graeme had never forgotten the soft texture of her skin. He'd lain awake more nights than he cared to remember, haunted by the memory of her limbs entwined with his own. Now, with her thigh thrown over his, it was all Graeme could do not to ease the fabric of the panties aside and thrust upward, to bury his aching shaft in her heat.

"Easy," he grunted. "I can't concentrate. There."

The bikini bottom sprang free and Lara lifted her hips as he slid the contraption down her legs, pulling her little booties from her feet at the same time. She stiffened for an instant as he tossed it all onto the floor, but relaxed when he came back up beside her and fastened his mouth to her breast.

In the next second, he'd unhooked the bra of the costume and tossed it onto the floor, and she was completely naked but for the golden mask that concealed her features, the glittering bracelets that encircled her arms, and the collar around her neck.

Graeme stroked a finger along the delicate line of her collarbone and drew it down between her breasts. Her breath hitched and she arched her spine, seeking closer contact with his hand.

"Christ, you're beautiful, La—Leia."

She stilled for a fraction of a second, and Graeme could have bitten his tongue off at his near slip. Had she noticed? He wasn't sure he could be with her and pretend she was a complete stranger to him. Not when he wanted to tear the goddamned mask from her face and shake her and demand to know why she was doing this, when for the past five years she hadn't ever—not once—tried to contact him.

Still another part of him wanted to thrust into her heat until they both came apart and she acknowledged that she belonged to him. He'd been her first. She'd always belong to him.

But he knew full well that he'd continue with the seductive farce, because he wanted her that much. If she wanted to pretend she was someone else, then he'd accommodate her.

For now.

There would be time later for revelations and recriminations. He didn't even care what her motivations were for coming back into his life, although he suspected she might only be interested in him because he was the face of Kip Corrigan. Most people he met seemed to have difficulty separating him from the fictional character he played on television. But right now, all he wanted was Lara, sweetly passionate beneath him, the way he'd dreamed so many times.

"Is that what you want to be called?" he asked, dipping his head to torment her nipple with his tongue. "Or do you want to give me your real name?"

"Leia," she gasped. "Call me Leia."

With a grunt of assent, Graeme slid a hand along the length of her thigh and over her hip. Her waist, always narrow, seemed more so now against the womanly flare of her buttocks and breasts. He wanted to look at her endlessly, to absorb all the details of her appearance in order to compare them mentally to his youthful memories of her.

Instead, he slid a hand over the smooth curve of her rear and between her thighs, easing a finger along her cleft. She was wet and ready for him, and the knowledge was like tossing fuel onto an open flame. He stroked her slick folds, tormenting the small rise of her clitoris until she clutched desperately at his shoulders and writhed against him.

"Oh, please." Her breath came in soft pants and her hips moved against his hand, seeking more of the intimate contact. "Please, I need—" She broke abruptly off and wound her arms around Graeme's neck and kissed him until he was breathless.

They were deep, openmouthed kisses that sent lust jackknifing through his midsection. She tasted of sweet Cointreau and pomegranate and Graeme was quickly becoming intoxicated.

Rolling her beneath him, he braced himself on one elbow and looked down at Lara's eyes behind the mask. They were foggy with desire, and her mouth was open and moist.

"Do you want this?" He couldn't bring himself to call her Leia; it would lend credence to her half-baked belief that he didn't know her. But he could damn well make sure she knew exactly who it was that was fucking her. "Do you?"

"Yes." She sighed and slid her hands over his back to cup his buttocks and urge him closer. "Yes, please."

Graeme didn't need to hear any more. Hooking his

hands behind her knees, he pushed her legs back until they were up by her breasts, and her feminine core was pressed against his pelvis. But he didn't take her.

Not yet.

Instead, he dragged his mouth down the center of her rib cage. Her chest heaved with her breathing, and as his lips traveled across her stomach, she quivered in response to his touch. Her hands tunneled through his hair, stroking his scalp and urging him on.

"Say my name," he muttered against her skin, and traced an intricate pattern around her navel with his tongue.

"Oh, oh…please," she gasped.

Graeme moved lower, rubbing his cheek across her mons before planting damp kisses along the sensitive skin of her inner thigh. Her scent was tantalizing. Heady. He breathed deeply before sweeping his tongue over her in one long, firm stroke, much as she had done to him.

She cried out and bucked her hips, but Graeme held her legs firmly in place. He softened the caress, swirling his tongue around the aroused bud of her clitoris, teasing it until he felt her muscles tighten with her impending orgasm. Lifting his face, he looked at her over the heaving landscape of her belly and breasts, to where her mask caught the light of the bedside table and flung shards of golden brilliance across the bedspread.

She was achingly beautiful.

"Say my name," he demanded. Releasing one leg, he eased a finger into her, feeling her muscles contract around him. "Say it."

Lara made an incoherent sound of pleasure and her

fingers knotted in his hair. Graeme withdrew his finger and waited. She glanced down at him and he could see distress warring with desire in her eyes.

"Graeme!"

The word was no more than a breathless exhale, but it was enough to satisfy him. Leaning over the edge of the bed, he snatched his pants from the floor and pulled his wallet from the back pocket, freeing a single condom from the billfold. Tearing it open between his teeth, he covered himself in one smooth movement, aware that Lara watched him from behind the glittering mask. Catching her once more beneath her knees, he surged over her.

"That's right," he agreed, staring down at her. "I'm Graeme Hamilton. But you already knew that, didn't you?"

His erection was poised at the entrance to her body, and his entire body ached with the need to bury himself inside her, yet he held back.

Lara stared at him for a moment, and then pressed her thighs tighter against his body. "Yes," she breathed. "I already knew that."

"Why are you here?" Graeme tensed in anticipation of her answer, not certain he was ready to hear whatever words came out of her delectable mouth, but needing her to say it just the same.

"Because I've fantasized about you." Her voice broke. "About this."

They were the last words Graeme had expected to hear, and they drove him over the edge of restraint. With a harsh sound of need, he captured Lara's lips with his own as he surged forward in one powerful motion, burying himself deep inside her. She was hot and tight, and made a whimpering sound as he withdrew and then thrust himself into her again.

"Damn," he muttered against her lips, "you're snug."

"You feel so good," she gasped, and clutched his back, her fingers digging into his muscles and her hips matching his rhythm.

Graeme gritted his teeth, not wanting to let go too soon. When Lara raised her legs and wrapped them around his hips, Graeme turned with her in his arms until he lay against the pillows and she straddled him.

"Ride me," he breathed, his hands on her hips. Behind the mask, he could see her confusion, and something in his chest shifted. Despite what she wanted him to believe, she was still innocent. "Just slide back and forth."

She shifted experimentally, and her lips parted on a surprised "Oh" of pleasure. Then, with one hand braced on his chest, she began to move back and forth, her thighs flexing with effort.

"That's it," Graeme purred, and held himself ruthlessly still, watching as Lara strove for her own release.

Beneath the bottom edge of the mask, she caught her lower lip between her small, white teeth. Her movements tormented him, drove him nearly wild with lust, but there was no way he'd hurry this. Each movement of her body caused her breasts to bounce invitingly.

She was the most beautiful thing he'd ever seen, and the collar and chain around her neck made him feel primal, possessive.

Graeme slid his hands to her hips and kneaded her buttocks, savoring the resiliency of her firm flesh before smoothing his palms over the fragile framework of her ribs to her breasts. He filled his hands with her and rubbed his thumbs across her nipples until she moaned and covered his fingers with her own.

He watched her face, wanting to pull the mask away so that he could see her expression, but she closed her eyes and concentrated on her pleasure. Graeme knew the precise instant when her climax washed over her. She shuddered and moaned, and her inner muscles contracted around him, squeezing him. Unable to hold back any longer, he grasped her hips to hold her still and with a harsh groan, came in a white-hot rush of pleasure.

Lara's breath came in hard pants, and her expression was one of sublime satisfaction. But when she opened her eyes and looked down at him, he saw something else there. Something soft and wanting, and it scared the hell out of him as much as it confused and infuriated him.

Instead of pulling her down into his arms, he disentangled himself from her limbs and sat up, swinging his legs to the floor and leaning forward to scrub his hands over his face.

"Don't move," he said grimly over his shoulder. "I'll clean up, and then we need to talk."

Less than five minutes later, Graeme pulled on a pair of jeans and nothing else and watched as Lara pushed the duvet to the bottom of the bed and dragged the sheet up over her nude body. With the mask still covering her face and the gold collar encircling her throat, she looked exotic.

Mysterious.

Even now, when his body should be sated by the amazing sex they'd just shared, he wanted her again.

Damn, he could use a stiff drink. Or a cigarette. But

he'd given up both years ago, when his degenerate life-style had threatened to consume him.

He rubbed a hand across the back of his neck and blew out a hard breath. "Let's talk."

Lara watched him from behind the mask. "Okay. But before we start talking, I just want you to know that I've never done anything like this before in my entire life."

"What? Had sex?" He gave a derisive snort. "I think we both know that's not true."

His voice sounded cynical, even to his own ears. Lara's eyes widened and Graeme could see the near panic in them. She was wondering if he'd guessed her identity.

He knew he should put an end to their little game, but something inside him wanted to torment her, just a little. "I mean, it's obvious you're not a virgin," he clarified. He should know, since five years ago she *had* been virginal, until he'd taken care of that.

Beneath the edge of the mask, her lips curved into a smile. "You're right, I'm not. But I meant that I haven't done *this* before. Gone back to a hotel room with a guy that I—that I hardly know."

Well, at least that was the truth. She might have known him once, but he wasn't that guy anymore. He'd changed in five years. If she had any illusions that he was still the same lovesick lad whom she could wrap around her finger, she had another surprise coming to her.

"So, what?" he asked laconically. "You're not into casual hook-ups?" He forced himself to sound careless; irreverent. Inwardly, his gut tightened just thinking about her with another guy.

"No," she replied. Behind the shadowed openings of the mask, her eyes shimmered. "At least, not before tonight."

"Well, that makes two of us then."

That, at least, was a partial truth. He hadn't done anything like this while he'd been sober enough to remember, and he hadn't had a drink in over three years.

Lara laughed softly, but Graeme thought it had a bitter edge to it. "Oh, come on. You don't have to say that on my account. After all, I know who you are. Women see you and make complete fools of themselves, even throwing their underwear at you. Nobody would blame you for taking what they offer."

Her words stung. Did she really believe he was so shallow as to screw a woman simply because she was attractive, or because she threw herself at him? Five years ago, he'd married Lara because he'd loved her and had been unwilling to sleep with her without the sanctity of marriage. He'd wanted her to know then that what they did together mattered to him. That he wouldn't simply use her for sex, no matter how much he wanted her.

And God knew he'd wanted her.

She'd been sweetly shy, but where he was concerned, she'd worn her heart on her sleeve. Her total lack of artifice was just one of the things about her that he'd found so appealing. She hadn't hidden the fact that she adored everything about him, and most of the time she'd looked at him as if he were her own personal hero. He could have had her at any time during that summer. She'd wanted him as much as he'd wanted her, but she'd been so innocent. So trusting. An incurable romantic who'd believed that eloping was the ultimate act of love. As tough as it had been, he'd wanted to wait until after they were legally married to make love to her.

It had only been in the months after she'd left him, when he'd finally accepted that she wouldn't be coming back, that he'd kicked aside his morals and tried to fill the aching void her absence had left by whatever method he could. Unable to control his black moods, his acting career had suffered. Even directors who knew him and worked with him in the past had refused to cast him in their productions. Embittered, he'd turned to alcohol and sex. Lots of alcohol and lots of meaningless sex that had done nothing to obliterate his memories of Lara and had left him feeling emptier than before.

It was true that now, all he had to do was appear in public and women came on to him, making their interest in him blatantly obvious. Initially, when his fame was still fairly new, he'd taken advantage of what they offered, but it had been a long time since he'd slept with any of the women he'd met in Hollywood or through the entertainment industry. The experiences always left him feeling as if he'd sacrificed a vital body part. In fact, most of the women he escorted to premieres and parties bored him to tears. With few exceptions, they were superficial and only interested in what might be in it for them. The fact that Lara thought him shallow enough to screw any woman who looked his way irritated the hell out of him.

"Is that what you think?" he demanded softly, bending toward her and bracing one hand on the headboard, aware his Scots brogue had thickened, a clear indication of his rising irritation. "That I'd fuck you simply because you begged for it? That all you have to do is throw your panties at me and I'll start drooling? That I have no control over myself? *Christ.*"

Graeme flung himself away from the bed with a snort of disgust, raking a hand over his hair. The worst part of it was that with Lara, he really did have no control over himself. He'd never had.

Even now, he wanted her again.

The fact that she was here dredged up emotions he'd thought he'd buried a long time ago. But the truth was, the fury and resentment he'd felt all those years ago, when Lara had chosen her family over him, were still very much alive. He'd just pushed the emotions aside and learned to ignore them.

But seeing Lara again was like opening an old wound that had festered for years and now exposed, felt raw and aching. He'd spent the last few years convincing himself that he was over her. The fact that she'd reappeared in his life and practically begged him to have sex with her should have made him feel smug. Victorious.

So why did he feel so miserable?

6

LARA WATCHED as Graeme turned away from her, distressed and puzzled by his reaction. The heat simmering through her body cooled a little beneath his contempt. But even as her apprehension grew, Lara couldn't help but admire Graeme as he strode toward the opposite side of the room. He was wearing nothing but a pair of unbuttoned jeans, and the muscles beneath the smooth, tawny skin bunched and flexed with his movements.

Lara couldn't believe what she had just done; she'd just had off-the-charts amazing sex with Graeme Hamilton. Whatever romantic memories she'd carried of the two nights they'd once spent together had just been obliterated beneath the powerful impact of his lovemaking.

Did she feel guilty for having slept with Graeme? Yes, but most of her guilt stemmed from the fact that she'd barely thought of Christopher while she'd been in Graeme's arms. That in itself was disturbing, since the whole reason she'd come to Las Vegas was to secure a divorce from Graeme so that she could take her relationship with Christopher to the next level.

What did she say about her as a person, if she could so easily betray somebody that she cared about? Another, more disturbing thought occurred to her; she knew without ever having slept with Christopher that sex with him would never be as good as it had just been with Graeme. But great sex wasn't enough to build a life around. Besides, she and Graeme had nothing in common and his lifestyle wasn't exactly suited to settling down.

Lara was twenty-three, and while most women her age might think that was way too young to start thinking about marriage and kids, Lara desperately wanted a family.

With her childhood spent shuffling between her mother in Chicago and her father in Washington—her father spending most of his time at work, her mother attending social events or plotting how she would ensnare her next husband—Lara had grown up lonely. Working with the children at the theatre had only reinforced her desire to settle down.

Christopher might not inspire her to grand passion, but she admired and respected him. They shared common interests. He treated her well and wanted her happiness. He'd make a good father and he'd be a faithful husband.

She would still ask Graeme to sign the divorce papers she'd brought with her. Then she would return to Chicago and pick up the pieces of her life, and she would never look back. But for tonight, at least, she'd get Graeme out of her system once and for all. She would gorge herself on him until she couldn't think about him without feeling a little sick.

She'd once done the same thing with toasted coconut marshmallows, eating six packages of them until she'd been so nauseous that she hadn't been able to get of bed. She hadn't had a craving for them since, and that had been fourteen years ago. Why should Graeme be any different? All she had to do was have sex with him until she felt too weak to move. When she finally reached the point where the sight of him made her feel boneless and queasy, then she'd know that she'd finally gotten him out of her system.

Now she watched as Graeme paced the hotel room. He scrubbed a hand over his hair and she could feel the frustration that rolled from him in waves. She could have kicked herself. Why did she have to go and ruin everything with her stupid comment about how she never indulged in one-night stands? She groaned inwardly. Even though he didn't know her identity, she'd wanted him to understand that casual sex that wasn't something she did.

Ever.

And the sex she'd just had with Graeme Hamilton had been anything but casual. It had been heated, intense and completely satisfying. But as she watched him pace the room, a chill of unease slowly replaced the delicious aftershocks of their explosive encounter. Lara dragged the sheet tighter around her body.

Clearly, her suggestion that he'd had his share of casual hookups had struck a nerve. But what was she supposed to think? That he'd been celibate since their ill-fated marriage? The very idea was ludicrous, and she didn't believe it.

He'd never denied the fact that he'd gone through a rough time in England before he'd been cast as the cocky bad-boy hero of *Galaxy's End*. He just hadn't revealed that his run of bad luck had coincided with the end of their whirlwind relationship. Stories still circulated the Internet about his lifestyle during those months—a lifestyle of drunken debauchery that had nearly gotten him killed on more than one occasion. Eventually, he'd pulled his life back together and had been cast in some small independent films before finding huge success in the role of Kip Corrigan.

If he'd had affairs since that time, who was she to judge him? After all, he'd had no idea they were still married at the time, and probably wouldn't have cared if he had known.

She knew how betrayed he'd felt when he'd discovered she'd lied to him about her age. And not just her age, but her identity, too. When she'd met him, she'd wanted him to like her for herself and not because she was Brent Whitfield's daughter. If she'd told him the truth—that she was seventeen years old and the daughter of the American Ambassador to England, he would have hightailed it in the opposite direction and she wouldn't have blamed him.

But she'd been certain, based on the fact that he was here with her now—without even knowing who she was—that he was no stranger to casual hookups. Dragging the sheet firmly around her, she slipped from the bed and crossed to where he stood with his back to her, and tentatively laid a hand against his bare skin. He flinched, but didn't turn around.

"I'm sorry," she offered. "I didn't mean to offend you. It's just that… Well, what was I supposed to think?" She gave a small huff of laughter. "I mean, here we are…complete strangers."

He turned around, his expression shuttered. "Not complete strangers."

Lara's breath hitched. "What do you mean?"

He took a step closer and closed his hands around her arms, his thumbs smoothing over her bare skin. "I mean that you already know who I am. So why don't you take off the mask and let me see you? We're only strangers as long as you hide yourself from me. And considering what we just shared…"

Lara relaxed marginally and gave him what she hoped was a convincingly sultry smile. "I'm not hiding myself from you. I mean, aside from my face, there isn't anything that you haven't already seen." Lara emphasized her words by loosening her grip on the sheet just enough to expose the upper curves of her breasts. "You already said I could keep the mask on, and…" She stopped, suddenly self-conscious.

"Yes?" Graeme prompted, his expression taut.

Unable to meet his eyes, Lara drew one finger down the center of his torso. "Well, I can think of so many things I'd rather do than talk. Just for tonight, let's pretend we have a…connection, like Kip and Lily. Let's pretend we're not strangers."

She thought briefly of the titillating episode from *Galaxy's End*, where Kip Corrigan, in an act of revenge, captured and enslaved Lily, the woman who had been his former jailer, aboard the prison ship. He'd shackled her to himself with a length of chain that ensured she'd have no privacy and no escape from his watchful eyes. But in the end, he'd been the one who'd suffered the most, when he realized that punishing his former guard was the last thing he wanted to do.

The love scene that had resulted from that reluctant attraction had been scorching. Video clips of the scene had flooded the Internet. The sensual encounter had inspired Lara to write several erotic tales in which she was able to fulfill her own bondage fantasies. Of course, in her imagination it was always Graeme and herself in the starring roles. One of her favorites involved him coming after her and forcibly abducting her. He would bind her to a bed then torment her with his hands and mouth until she begged him for release. Just the thought of being bound to Graeme that way made her insides turn to mush.

"Is that what this is to you, then? A game of make-believe?" His voice was low, his accent more pronounced. "I hate to disappoint you, love, but I'm not Kip Corrigan."

Unsure of his mood, Lara risked a glance at his face. He watched her intently, his eyes more green than blue. A muscle flexed in his jaw.

"I don't want Kip Corrigan," she finally said. "I want you, and I would never have had the nerve to come on to you in the elevator like that except that—"

She broke off abruptly as Graeme stepped closer. The sheet slipped from her nerveless fingers to crumple on the ground between them. Graeme's eyes darkened as they drifted over her.

"Except that?" His voice was low, little more than a growl.

"Except that you looked at me like you wanted to devour me." Her voice was oddly breathless. She reached out a hand and traced a finger over his abs. "Like you wanted me, right then and there. Like I could bring your fantasies to life, and maybe a few of my own, too."

One tiny step brought her flush against him. Her breasts brushed his chest and beneath the rough fabric of his jeans she could feel the hot thrust of his erection.

Lara thrilled at the knowledge that she could affect him that way. Leaning forward, she skated her lips over the strong line of his collarbone, and slid her hand lower on his abdomen, until her fingers brushed against the open fly of his pants.

His stomach muscles tightened beneath her touch, and Lara heard his breathing hitch. But before she could take advantage of his involuntary response, he grasped her wrist and halted her downward exploration.

"Stop."

Lara swallowed the trepidation that rose in her throat, and nuzzled his strong neck, tasting him with small flicks of her tongue. "Do you really want me to stop? The night's still young, and there's so much I could still do for you…"

To her shock, he pushed her gently away from him. He scrubbed his hands over his face. Feeling utterly exposed, Lara retrieved the sheet from where she'd dropped it and dragged it around her nakedness, pushing down the apprehension that slithered through her.

"What's wrong?" she asked.

Graeme swiped a hand across his face and turned partially away from her with a disbelieving laugh, before swinging back around. "Jesus, how can you— I can't keep doing this."

Lara's dread grew. "Doing what?"

He swore softly and then grabbed her by the upper arms and hauled her upward until she was standing almost on tiptoe, his face less than an inch from her own, and suddenly Lara knew that her mask wasn't nearly enough to protect her.

"I know who you are, Lara," he ground out, and released her so abruptly that she staggered.

She took two steps backward, still clutching the sheet against her breasts, until her thighs bumped against the mattress. Blood thudded hotly through her veins as she stared at him in mute horror, and yet she still tried to prolong the inevitable.

"I—I don't know what you're talking about."

He advanced on her then, his face taut and his eyes glittering with intent. Lara sat down abruptly on the bed and watched him approach. But it wasn't until he loomed over her and his hands moved with unerring accuracy to the clasp at the back of her head that she was galvanized into action.

"No, don't!" Dropping the sheet, her hands closed around his strong wrists, but it was too late. In the next instant, the mask was gone and there was nothing left for her to hide behind.

7

"LARA."

She stared at him with those wide, sapphire eyes and a swift, fierce heat swept through his body. Graeme dropped the mask onto the floor, uncaring where it landed. He couldn't drag his gaze away from Lara's upturned face, registering the small changes that five years had accomplished. Where her body had blossomed and filled out, her face had lost the roundness of girlhood, her cheekbones were more pronounced than he remembered. A tiny scar marred the smoothness of her forehead.

But her mouth hadn't changed a bit.

Still overly full and lush, her lips completely distracted him. His fixation was broken when she reached down and dragged the sheet back up to cover her nakedness.

"How?" she croaked. "How did you know it was me?"

"Did you really think I wouldn't recognize you?" He couldn't keep the disbelief out of his voice. "That I wouldn't immediately know who you were?"

Her breath hissed in. "You knew it was me? The whole time? Back in the elevator, you knew?"

"Even before then. I knew the instant I saw you in the ballroom."

Twin patches of color bloomed on Lara's cheeks. She tried to stand up, but Graeme kept her in place with one foot planted firmly on the trailing edge of the sheet, allowing her no slack. If she wanted to stand, she would have to release the bed linen.

"How could you?" Her voice was shaky with indignation and, Graeme suspected, embarrassment. "How could you let me go on like that? How could you go on pretending that you had no idea who I was?"

Graeme's pulse thudded hard and hot through his veins, and the urge to drag Lara to her feet and shake her was almost irresistible. It was either that or kiss her. Unwilling to let her see how strongly she affected him, he took refuge instead in sarcasm.

"I'm a man, Lara. How could I not let you continue? Especially when you seemed to be enjoying yourself so much?"

Lara drew in a sharp breath, and beneath the protective barrier of the sheet, her chest rose and fell rapidly. Good. He hoped she felt insulted. He told himself that he wanted her to feel miserable.

"Well, then," she said tartly, "based on your response, I'd say that makes two of us."

Oh, yeah. He'd enjoyed every sensual second of their steamy encounter, but there was no way he'd admit it. Not to her. Not yet. Not until he'd figured out exactly what she was up to.

"Sweetheart, I make a living out of pretending. But you definitely missed your calling." He couldn't keep the derision from his voice. "If you ever decide to give acting a try, let me know and I'll set you up with my agent. Hollywood is always looking for women who can fake it."

Lara pushed at him until he stepped back, and she shot to her feet. Her eyes narrowed on him, but Graeme saw the telltale sheen of moisture in them and something in his chest shifted. He'd struck a chord. He told himself he didn't care, but his hands fisted at his sides in an effort to keep from reaching for her.

He'd thought of being with her again so often, but he'd never imagined that she'd come to him in disguise, that she wouldn't want him to know who she was. Worse, that she would want him to pretend that he was somebody other than himself.

For the first time since he'd taken on the role of bad boy Kip Corrigan, Graeme found himself resenting the fictional character. He strongly suspected that Lara was more enamored of Kip than she was of him.

"Is that what you think?" she demanded softly. "That I *faked* it?"

They stared at each other for a long moment. Her eyes were wide, the pupils hugely dilated, her breathing uneven.

"No," Graeme finally bit out, searching her eyes. "I think your...performance was real enough. What I want to know is *why?* Why now, after all these years, are you suddenly interested in renewing our...relationship?"

He watched the expressions that briefly twisted her features; grief, anger and then something that looked suspiciously like regret. "Because what I said earlier was true."

Graeme frowned. "Refresh my memory."

She tipped her chin up and held his gaze, and for a moment Graeme thought she wouldn't answer. Then she lowered her lashes, fixing her attention somewhere on his midriff, and hot color swept up from beneath the edge of the sheet, mottling her chest and neck.

"I said I'd fantasized about you," she finally mumbled. "About being with you."

Graeme snorted in disbelief. "Don't you mean that you've fantasized about being with Kip Corrigan?"

He watched as the color drained from her face. "Why would you say that?"

Graeme paused. He wanted to say more, to tell her that he knew damned well it was Kip and not himself that she wanted, but seeing her expression, he took pity on her. "Forget it. You were saying?"

Lara drew in a deep breath. "I didn't come to the convention with the intention of doing…this. Not exactly, anyway." She twisted her hands in the fabric of the sheet. "I thought I might have a chance to talk with you, because there's something I need to tell you. But then I saw you on stage, and I realized it had been a mistake to come here, that I didn't have the courage to face you. So I left the ballroom, but you followed me." She made a helpless gesture with one hand. "Then you didn't recognize me, and the costume shop sent me the wrong costume, but it didn't matter because it made me feel— Made me feel—"

"Made you feel…what?"

She raised her gaze to his, and her eyes shimmered. "Made me feel like the sexiest woman in the world."

Graeme's pulse became a hot, insistent thudding in his veins. He wanted nothing more than to close the distance between them, drag the sheet from her body, and prove to her that she was, indeed, the sexiest woman in the world, at least in his eyes. But he'd already let her sidetrack him once, and he wasn't about to lose control again without knowing her reasons for being there. "So if you didn't set out to screw me blind—in a literal sense—then why did you come?"

He watched as Lara drew in a deep breath and the flush of color climbed into her face. She gave him a look that silently begged him not to do this. "I *had* to. There's something you have to know... I'm sorry." She laughed, but it had a bitter sound to it. "Believe it or not, this is one of the most difficult things I've ever had to say. You'll be angry."

Anger did sweep through Graeme, fierce and swift. He was such a fool. He'd actually thought that maybe—just maybe—Lara had come back to him because she wanted him. Because she'd missed him, maybe even as much as he'd missed her. But seeing the resignation and regret in her eyes, he realized nothing could be further from the truth. His gut told him that what he'd suspected was true; she'd sought him out because she wanted a divorce.

"Just tell me why you came." His voice was low and tight and her expression was miserable, but he didn't care. He'd be damned if he'd make it easy for her.

"Because my father died a couple of weeks ago."

Whatever he'd expected her to say, that wasn't it. The news shocked him, but he couldn't deny feeling a savage satisfaction upon hearing that Brent Whitfield was dead. The arrogant son of a bitch had single-handedly destroyed his life five years earlier. But then he looked at Lara's face and saw the grief etched there.

"I'm sorry," he said stiffly.

"Thank you." She drew in a deep, hard breath. "He'd been sick for some time, but it wasn't until after he'd... passed...that his lawyers gave me a letter he'd written to me."

"Go on."

Lara glanced at him, then quickly away. "I'm not sure…it doesn't really even matter, because you've never expressed a desire to get married again." Her gaze flicked to him again. "At least, not publicly. I mean, if you *had*, then I'm sure my father would have told you that we're still—that is, we're not—that our marriage was never—"

"What? Never annulled?"

"You know?" Her face expressed her utter shock. "That we're still married?"

"Of course I know. I refused to sign your father's damned annulment papers." Graeme couldn't keep the contempt out of his voice. "Whatever influence your father might have had in Washington did *not* extend to me. I told him then that if you wanted out of this marriage, you'd need to tell me so yourself. To my face."

Lara had gone pale. "All these years, and you knew. Why—"

Graeme put up a hand to forestall her from speaking. "If you're going to try and tell me that you didn't know we were still legally married, then you've taken me for an even bigger fool than your father did."

Lara made a soft gasping sound. "I *didn't* know. I thought the marriage was annulled five years ago." Her voice vibrated with indignation and dismay. "I was…estranged from my father for years before he died."

Graeme snorted. "Sure. Pretty damned convenient that he's dead and you've suddenly discovered we're still married. Why don't you just admit it? You were too much of a coward to stand up to him when he was alive, but now that he's gone, you're wondering if we can pick up where we left off, is that it? Well, I'm sorry to break it to you, love, but too much damned water has passed beneath that bridge."

Lara shook her head, and if her bemusement wasn't genuine, she did a pretty good job faking it. Graeme refused to let her appalled expression soften the edge of his anger.

"C'mon," he jeered softly. "You're here because now that your father's dead, there isn't anyone to prevent you from doing whatever you want. Maybe you thought it would be fun to screw with my head a little more, is that it? You could live out your private fantasy of sleeping with Kip Corrigan, and then go back to your exclusive, exalted lifestyle, and nobody would ever be the wiser, including me. Have I got it right?"

Lara blanched, and Graeme had a moment of doubt before he determinedly pushed it down. After all, he *knew* her secret.

"I would never try to—to *use* you that way." Her tone sounded sincere enough, but her gaze slid away from his, making him wonder how close he'd come to the truth.

He arched an eyebrow. "Oh, really?"

She flushed. "No. How could you even think that?"

"Oh, I don't know." His voice grew hard. "Maybe because you have a history of lying to me."

"Oh, that's unfair! I tried to explain to you why I lied about my age that summer in London. I was afraid you wouldn't want me if you knew the truth!"

"And you'd have been right." He all but snarled the words, even as he silently acknowledged that he'd have taken her on any terms. "But that wasn't all you lied to me about, Lara. Our entire relationship was based on lies. Your age, your name, your background—it was all a big game to you, wasn't it? You were nothing but a spoiled-rotten brat who would have said and done anything to get your way. Why should I think anything has changed?"

"That's *not* how it was, and you know it." Her voice broke, and she bent swiftly to scoop up the bits and pieces of her scattered costume, but not before Graeme saw the sheen of tears in her eyes. "I *loved* you."

Loved him.

The past tense wasn't lost on Graeme and he couldn't keep the weary resignation out of his voice. "And yet, here you are again, trying to deceive me about who you really are."

She snapped upright, and now twin flags of color rode high on her cheekbones and her eyes held a dangerous glitter. "If that's really what you think, then we have nothing more to discuss."

"Discuss?" he repeated. "I wasn't aware you were interested in *talking*."

"I'm not!" she snapped. "At least, not anymore." She swept him with one angry glance. "I see some things haven't changed. You're still as proud as always. And still unwilling to recognize the truth, even when it's right under your nose."

"And what would that truth be?" He took a step toward her. His voice was low and fierce, and vibrated with an anger he couldn't suppress. "Tell me right now that you don't want something from me. Tell me that if I weren't the face of Kip Corrigan, you'd still be here."

Lara squared her shoulders and glared at him,

clutching the ridiculous metal bikini against her breasts. "You know, I think fame and fortune have gone to your head, Graeme. I actually don't know why I'm still here. But you're right about one thing— I do want something from you."

They were interrupted by the sudden, strident ringing of the telephone on the bedside table. For a moment, neither of them moved, then Graeme snatched the receiver from the cradle.

"What?" he snapped.

"Where the hell are you?" Tony shouted. "Why haven't you answered your cell phone? I've been trying to call you for over an hour. You do realize that you have obligations to this festival, don't you? Don't pull a vanishing act on me now, Graeme. You have two separate autograph signings tomorrow, and don't forget that you have an interview on KXNT television in the morning."

Graeme listened for a scant instant to the loud, angry voice on the other end, and then turned to Lara, holding up one finger to indicate they weren't yet finished. "My publicist again," he explained shortly. "Don't move. We're not through here."

He turned away from Lara to speak quietly into the phone, but a movement from her made him turn around. Before he could realize her intent, she'd dragged the trailing end of the sheet around her, toga-style. With her head held high, unmindful of the chunky slave collar around her neck or her bare feet, she swept out of the bedroom.

"Lara!" he called, then swore and dropped the phone back into its cradle, abruptly silencing the furious voice on the other end. Graeme strode through the bedroom, but it wasn't until he heard the outer hotel-room door slam that he realized she had left.

In disbelief, he raked both hands through his hair, then muttered a savage curse as he realized he'd done the one thing he'd sworn he would never do again; he'd let her go. But this time, she wouldn't get away so easily.

8

THE DAMNED, arrogant, conceited man. If she had any sense, she'd book the first fight back to Chicago. Seeing Graeme again had been a huge mistake. She'd completely underestimated just how attractive she still found him. She couldn't do this herself.

If she was smart, she'd call her attorney and have him take care of serving Graeme with the divorce papers. She'd never so much as look at him again. But when it came to Graeme, Lara had never had any sense.

She couldn't even think about what had happened in his hotel room without turning hot, and then icy-cold. Mortification swamped her each time she thought about what they'd done, which was approximately every millisecond since she'd left his room.

Wearing nothing but a bed sheet and a slave collar.

She didn't know which was worse—Graeme's insinuation that she was only after him for sex, or the scandalous glances she'd received while riding the elevator down to her own room. Worse, there'd been no hiding her face from the other curious guests. She'd left the gorgeous Venetian mask behind. She'd been in such a hurry to get out of there that she'd grabbed her boots and the costume, but had somehow missed the gold mask.

Well, fine. He could keep it.

Despite the fact that it was almost midnight by the time she returned to her room, she turned on the shower and stood beneath the steaming jet for a full twenty minutes, letting the hot spray soothe her frayed nerve endings. There was no way she could sleep.

All she could think about was how right it had felt to be in his arms again. She'd missed him even more than she wanted to admit. And the things he'd done… She could still feel the hard heat of his body against her own, feel his breath against her neck, hear the deep, masculine sounds of satisfaction he made as he drove into her. A fresh wave of fire coursed through her.

If she was smart, she'd leave now and put as much distance as possible between herself and Graeme. She'd already demonstrated that she couldn't be near the guy without losing her head. But she knew she wouldn't leave. She didn't have that kind of self-discipline.

She was worse than pathetic.

Stepping out of the shower, Lara toweled herself dry and dragged a comb through her wet hair. She tugged on a T-shirt and panties.

She was deliciously tender in spots, especially where his rough jaw had abraded the sensitive skin of her breasts and her inner thighs. If she closed her eyes, she could still feel Graeme's hands on her, still feel him surging into her, still see the expression on his face as he'd made love to her.

He'd known it was her.

The thought made her pause. He'd known all along it was her. He'd invited her back to his room and practically consumed her, *knowing full well who she was.*

The implications stunned her as much as they scared the life out of her. He was too perceptive, by far. He'd always known how her mind worked. Sometimes she'd thought that he understood her better than she understood herself.

She'd been writing stories since she was young, and that summer in London had been no different. She'd thought Graeme might find her efforts humorous, especially when she told him that the story she'd been working on was a fantasy romance. Instead, he'd been sincerely interested and wanted to read what she'd written. Letting him take her manuscript home with him was the hardest thing she'd ever done and she'd spent most of that night pacing and fretting. Would he mock her writing? Scoff at her efforts? Or worse, would he read between the lines and realize how desperately she longed to be loved like her heroine?

But he hadn't mocked her work. He'd told her in all seriousness how much he'd enjoyed reading her story, and that he had a few suggestions on how she might make her intimate scenes with the hero more realistic, and her fight scenes with the villain ring true. Lara had fallen in love with him in that moment.

Knowing her as he did, maybe he'd guessed that she could only seduce him if she believed her identity to be secret. Maybe he'd thought that if he confronted her, she'd just run away again. She'd always been good at *that*.

Graeme had been right; she *had* been too much of a coward to stand up to her father all those years ago. But she liked to think that her reasons for leaving Graeme hadn't been purely selfish.

Her father had told her, in painful detail, what life would be like if she chose to stay with Graeme. As a struggling actor, he wouldn't be able to provide adequately for her. She would have to find a job. Without her father's financial support, attending college would be an impossibility, but without an education, her employment opportunities would be limited. Graeme would hate seeing her working in retail or the service industry. He'd give up his dream of acting in order to find a "real" job, and eventually he'd come to resent her.

On some level, Lara had known her father spoke the truth, but she'd found herself unable to sign the annulment papers he'd thrust at her. If her father wanted to file the papers himself, that was his right, at least for two more weeks, until she turned eighteen, but there was no way she could willingly put an end to what had been the happiest time in her life.

Her father had been furious, and had promised he would file the annulment paperwork as her guardian, but obviously things hadn't gone as planned.

She couldn't help but wonder why Graeme had never tried to contact her during the past five years. He'd known they were still married, yet he'd apparently made no effort to file for divorce, or to end their legal relationship. The thought gave Lara hope.

Glancing at the bedside clock, she saw it was just past midnight. She desperately needed someone to talk to, to help her make sense of the bungled mess she'd just made of everything. There was no way she could call Christopher; he thought she was in North Carolina, grieving for her father. Nor was there any way she could tell him that she'd come to Las Vegas to seek a divorce from her onetime husband who, by the way, she'd just had seriously hot sex with. Nope. But she could call the one person she'd trust with her secrets.

Before she could change her mind, she retrieved her cell phone and punched in Val's number, waiting impatiently for her friend to pick up.

"Lara?" Val's voice was alert, and in the background, Lara could hear music and noisy conversation. "Why are you calling so late? Are you okay?"

Lara frowned. "Yes, at least I think so. What is that commotion? Where are you? It's after midnight."

"Hang on a minute, hon." A moment later, the background noise was reduced to a distant hum. "Sorry about that. I'm at Molly Flanagan's."

Lara recognized the name of the Irish pub that she and Christopher sometimes frequented, along with other staff members from the nonprofit theater company. But Val rarely ever joined them in the evenings, preferring a more sophisticated night scene.

"You're at Molly Flanagan's?" Lara repeated.

"I'm with the theater staff," Val said. "We're just getting ready to leave. But what's up with you? Did you go to the masquerade ball? Did you see *him?*"

Lara closed her eyes and drew in a deep breath. "Val, I *slept* with him."

There was a moment of stunned silence on the other end of the phone. "Come again?"

Lara groaned at her friend's poor choice of words. "Yes, well, that's not likely to happen. I only did it because I didn't think he'd recognize me. You said yourself that I've changed in five years."

"Lara, I meant that in a figurative sense, not a literal one."

"Now you tell me," Lara groaned. "Val, I'm so confused! I don't know what to do."

Val's voice sharpened. "What do you mean? You're not going to ask for the divorce?"

"No, no," Lara said, twirling a wet strand of hair around one finger. "In spite of the sex, I don't think he even likes me. He acts like he totally despises me. I've made such a mess of everything. I think I'm just going to come home."

There was a brief silence. "Talk to him first, Lara. You know you have a wild imagination. Maybe he doesn't really hate you, and that's just your guilt talking. You told Christopher you'd be gone for at least four or five days. He'll think it's strange if you come back so soon."

In the background, Lara heard a man's voice call Val's name.

"Who was that?" she asked. "It sounded like Christopher."

"Yes, it's him," Val said, in a voice so resigned that Lara could almost see her rolling her eyes. "We're getting ready to leave and he's probably wondering why I'm outside, and not with the rest of the group. You know how he is, always looking out for everyone."

"Oh, well, don't let him know you're talking to me," she begged. "He'll think something's wrong if I'm calling so late, and I don't want him to worry. And whatever you do, please, *please* don't tell him where I am or what I just did. He'd never forgive me."

"I won't say a thing," Val promised. "Listen, I have to go. Sure you're okay?"

"Yes. I'm fine. Have fun."

"Talk to Graeme, okay?" Val's voice was low. "I'm

sure the two of you can come to an agreement like civilized adults."

"Sure. I'll talk with him."

Lara snapped the cell phone shut, feeling like her world was even more upside-down than before. Valerie worked in Chicago's fast-moving fashion industry, and although she treated Christopher with courtesy, Lara knew the two of them didn't always see eye to eye. Christopher thought Valerie was frivolous and shallow, and she'd always referred to him as good-looking, but stuffy. Lara couldn't envision Val hanging out with Christopher and the rest of the theater staff at an Irish pub.

At that moment, a loud knock sounded on her hotel room door, startling her. Her first thought was that Graeme had tracked her down, and her heart rate kicked into overdrive.

"Who's there?" she called.

"Hotel security, ma'am," came a female voice. "I have a package here for you."

A package? Lara approached the door and stood on tiptoe to peek through the peephole. Sure enough, a woman wearing a security uniform stood patiently on the other side of the door holding a white plastic bag in her hands. It looked suspiciously like a hotel laundry bag.

"I'm not expecting a package," Lara called, recalling the security training her father had drilled into her from the time she was small. "Leave it at the front desk and I'll get it in the morning."

"I'm sorry, Ms. Whitfield," the woman replied, "but I was told this had to be delivered to you personally. Tonight. It's from Mr. Hamilton."

Lara closed her eyes briefly. "Fine," she muttered, and withdrawing the chain, she opened the door. "I'll take it," she said, and held out her hand for the bag.

To her astonishment, the woman stepped back with an apologetic smile, and Graeme himself stepped away from the wall next to her door. Lara's jaw dropped, and she tried hastily to close the door, but it was too late. Graeme put his foot squarely against it.

"Thank you, Marissa," he said to the security guard. "I owe you."

The woman simpered up at him. "My pleasure, Mr. Hamilton." She handed the bag to Graeme and her eyes flicked to Lara. "I'm sorry, ma'am. I hope you two manage to work things out."

As Lara watched, the woman turned and walked back down the corridor toward the elevators. Graeme put a hand on the door and raised an eyebrow at Lara.

"Are you going to let me in, or shall we do this in the hallway, where every other guest on the floor can hear us?" he asked quietly.

Grudgingly, Lara stepped back and allowed him to enter. He still wore the jeans—buttoned closed, thank goodness—and a black T-shirt emblazoned with the words Everyone's an Actor. A pair of flip-flop sandals were on his feet.

"That was pretty low," she said, closing the door behind him. "Is that how you operate? You just smile and charm the women, and they give you whatever you want?"

"Pretty much," he agreed.

He stood in the center of her room, and Lara knew his eyes missed nothing. The bedsheet that she'd taken from his room still lay in a crumpled heap outside the bathroom door, along with the discarded remnants of her Princess Leia costume. He considered them for a moment before he turned and handed her the bag.

"You forgot your mask."

Lara crossed her arms over her chest, acutely aware of her wet hair and that fact that she wore only a T-shirt and a pair of panties.

"I don't want you here," she said, but she couldn't meet his eyes.

"Well, that's too bad," he said softly, and dropped the bag onto the surface of the desk. "Because we still have unfinished business."

Lara raised her eyes to his, and her breathing quickened at the raw emotion she saw reflected there. Anger simmered deep in their translucent depths, and something else, too, that she couldn't identify.

"What—what do you mean?" Her voice came out sounding very small.

He smiled, but it didn't reach his eyes. "Even after all these years, you haven't changed, love. You still have a very bad habit of running away when things get unpleasant."

Lara swallowed hard and waited.

"Before you left," he continued softly, "you said there was something you wanted from me, and I'd like to know what that is."

Lara uncrossed her arms and pushed past him. Bending over, she scooped up the scattered bits of costume and shoved them back into the empty envelope that still lay on her bed from when she'd unpacked it earlier that night. She needed to do something—anything—to distract her. He was too big. Too male.

Too completely tempting.

"Have you forgotten?" he asked from behind her.

She paused in her actions, but didn't turn around. "No. I haven't forgotten."

"Then tell me what it is you want."

Lara did turn around then, hugging the bulky envelope against her chest, disarmed by his nearness. She hadn't heard him approach, and he stood directly in front of her. He had one hand braced on her bedside table, and Lara realized with a sense of horror that her silver locket—the one he had given her on their wedding night—rested less than an inch from his fingertips.

Had he seen it? Would he remember it if he did? Surely he wouldn't attach any significance to the fact that she still had the locket. He didn't need to know that she wore it every day. She wished now that she hadn't brought it with her.

She dragged her gaze back to his face. He watched her intently, and suddenly she wasn't sure if she could say the words. They stuck in her throat, choking her.

"Tell me, love," he urged, his voice deceptively soft. "What do you want from me?"

"A divorce," she whispered brokenly. "I want a divorce."

SOMETHING TORE free in Graeme's chest with a harsh, wrenching pain. He'd instinctively known that this was the reason she'd come back, the only reason she'd come looking for him. Not because she'd missed him, not because her father had died and there was no longer any reason for her to stay away.

She wanted him out of her life.

Despite knowing that this day would come, and despite trying to prepare himself, Graeme felt as if he'd been punched hard in the solar plexus.

He studied Lara's face for a long moment. Her skin had taken on a blotchy appearance and her blue eyes shimmered with an unnatural brightness, as if she was close to tears. He noted the way she gnawed her lower lip in agitation, and how her pulse beat frantically at the base of her neck. That tiny disturbance captured his attention and completely distracted him.

But even if she'd been able to hide her anxiety from him, Graeme had already seen enough to realize that she wasn't unaffected by him. Not even close.

He'd spotted the stack of magazines on her table, along with the issue of *People* magazine that sported his photo on the cover. That in itself hadn't struck him as significant. But the necklace was another matter altogether.

As soon as he saw it on her bedside table, he felt his heart give an odd twist. He'd wanted to give her something to remember him by after she returned to the States, so he'd bought the locket and filled it with photos of the two of them.

But she hadn't wanted to return to the States without him. He would have gone willingly with her to the ends of the earth, that's how in love with her he'd been. In fact, he had already decided to return to America with her, but she'd insisted that they needed to get married first.

To elope.

He'd suspected then that her family might not approve of him, and although he hadn't been crazy about the idea of getting married in such a hurry, she'd been insistent. So sweetly insistent, in fact, that he'd found himself in Scotland, standing before a minister, before he fully realized the implications of what they'd done.

Not that he'd regretted it. Not for an instant. He'd given her the locket that night, before they'd made love for the first time. He could still recall how it had looked, sliding between her breasts, and the fierce pride and possessiveness he'd felt in finally claiming her as his own.

"So you want a divorce," he finally managed to say.

"Yes." Her voice was low, little more than a whisper.

"So what was that, back in my room? Breakup sex? Something to soften the blow? A consolation prize?" He couldn't keep the bitterness out of his voice.

Lara tipped her chin up. "I didn't know we were married until a few weeks ago, or I would have sought the divorce sooner. But if you must know, there's— there's somebody else." She flushed. "Somebody I'm serious about."

The thing in Graeme's chest tightened, fisting itself hard around his heart. "I see. He's given you a ring then, has he?" He dropped his gaze deliberately to her hands where they clutched the envelope, taking in her bare fingers. She wore no jewelry, nor were there any telltale marks on her ring finger to indicate she might have worn one.

To his satisfaction, Lara placed the envelope onto the bedside table—directly on top of the necklace—and pushed her hands behind her back. He didn't mind one bit, since the movement caused her breasts to thrust forward beneath the thin fabric of her T-shirt. He could clearly make out the outline of her nipples and as he watched, they hardened into twin points of perfection.

"He hasn't actually asked me to marry him," Lara

mumbled. "*Yet*. But I'm sure that he will. Soon. And I want to be unencumbered when he does."

"Ah." Graeme let all the derision and contempt he felt for the other man drip from his voice. "Is that what I am, then? An encumbrance?"

"I can hardly accept his marriage proposal while I'm still legally wed to you, can I?" she asked. "So yes, I guess that makes you an encumbrance. But then, I doubt you want to be married to me, either. I mean, look at you. You're the number-one fantasy on the mind of every woman between the ages of fourteen and—and a hundred and fourteen!"

With a huff of annoyance, she made to move away from him, but he caught her arm. She glanced up at him in alarm, and Graeme forced himself to keep his expression shuttered. No way did he want her to guess how much her words affected him.

"And what about you, love? Am I the number-one fantasy on your mind?"

Lara swallowed hard and he thought he saw an expression of longing flitter across her features. Then it was gone.

"Don't be ridiculous," she muttered. "I may have lived in a fantasy world when I was a little girl, but I'm all grown-up now. I need more than fantasies to keep me happy, Graeme."

"So I take it you're not writing anymore?"

She grew still and stared at him. "What is that supposed to mean?" she asked.

"I only meant that five years ago you were happy enough writing fantasy stories. Don't tell me you've given up writing?"

"I still write," she finally admitted, "but the stories

aren't for publication. They're for a—a unique audience."

"Ah," he said, filling his voice with meaning. "So you write strictly for your own *pleasure,* do you?"

Lara eyed him warily. "Yes, as a matter of fact, I do."

"You let me read your writing once." He arched an eyebrow at her.

She swallowed hard. "Yes, well, those days are gone."

"So nobody reads what you write these days?"

"I didn't say that, but if you're asking me to share my stories with you, then the answer is no." She gave her arm a tug and Graeme released her. "My stories have changed since the days when I let you read them. You'd be shocked."

"Really? In what way?"

"It doesn't matter. Suffice to say they're still fantasies, and I'd rather keep them private."

"Ah, but you haven't completely given up on fantasies," he pressed, enjoying her discomfort. *Or kept them private,* he thought.

"Maybe not," she admitted, "but at least I no longer expect them to come true."

Graeme remembered a time when both he and Lara had lived in a fantasy world, and he'd been her knight in shining armor. He'd thought that they would have their happily ever after, but it had turned out to be nothing more than a badly written fairy tale. He didn't mind so much for himself. He was accustomed to a certain amount of disillusionment.

He'd grown up in the tough south-side neighborhood of Glasgow. His mother had worked three jobs so that she could send Graeme and his brother to the exclusive Glasgow Academy, rather than the inner-city school near their home.

Graeme had been thirteen, and he still remembered how excited he had been on that first day of class. But he and his brother hadn't been welcomed by the other boys at the school, and before the week was through, Graeme had been involved in three fights.

Worse, the boys from the south-side neighborhood had taunted them as they'd arrived home each day in their Academy uniforms. Graeme might have been able to ignore them if he had been by himself, but when they'd begun pushing his younger brother around, he'd seen red and beaten one of the boys bloody. A week later, he'd been expelled from the Academy and forced to return to public school. He'd struggled and worked hard, and had managed to put himself through the Royal Academy of Dramatic Arts, but he'd seen the worst side of human nature along the way.

Disillusionment had been part of his life for as long as he could remember, but to see Lara—sweet, idealistic Lara—speak with such disenchantment, caused his chest to tighten.

He pulled her toward him, seeing the wariness in her eyes. "Let me make you happy, love," he said, his voice low and husky. "I can make you happy."

Sliding a hand beneath her damp hair, he cupped the soft nape of her neck and tipped her face up, his eyes raking her flushed features. She exhaled softly and her lashes fluttered, and Graeme bent his head to cover her lips with his own.

9

FOR JUST an instant, Lara stood stiff and unresponsive in his arms. Then she made an incoherent sound of need and wound her arms around his neck, her fingers tunneling through his hair and holding him still as she kissed him back.

And she didn't just kiss him. She devoured him. Her lips were soft and urgent, her tongue warm and sweet against his own.

"I know," she whispered into his mouth. "I know you can make me happy."

Her husky admission obliterated the miniscule vestiges of control he'd struggled to retain since he'd first entered her room. He'd promised himself that he wouldn't do or say anything to make her run away again, but he needed to know why she'd sought him out, why she'd given herself to him.

Being in her hotel room with her reminded him of the weekend that they'd eloped. They'd booked a room at a small Scottish inn and hadn't come out for two days. In fact, if Lara's father hadn't found them and forcibly dragged Lara from his arms, he'd bet they could have happily stayed in that room for a week or more without ever coming out.

Now here he was, surrounded by her belongings,

with her familiar scent filling his senses, and feeling for the first time in a long time that he was where he belonged. Seeing the silver locket had made him realize that he'd been a part of her life for the past five years, whether he'd realized it or not. She hadn't forgotten him.

Now, with a hoarse groan, he hauled her against his body, feeling the soft crush of her breasts against his chest. He slanted his mouth over hers, knowing he needed to slow down and do this right, but too desperate to claim her as his own now that she'd dropped all pretenses. He'd thought of her—wanted her—for too long. He'd kept his distance for five years—no longer.

Lara's hands were frantically working the button on his pants, hastily and inexpertly, with none of the finesse or teasing she'd demonstrated just an hour or two before.

"Easy," he breathed against her mouth. "Here…let me."

With their lips still fused, he released the fastening at his waistband. Lara hummed in approval as she slid her hand beneath his jeans and cupped him in her palm.

Groaning heavily, Graeme dragged his mouth from Lara's and pressed his lips against the tender skin beneath her ear. His breathing sounded harsh in the quiet room. Lust ricocheted through his gut, and he wanted nothing more than to strip her clothes from her body, drag her to the floor and consume her. The sheer ferocity of his thoughts shocked him, and he forced himself to slow down and gentle his touch.

"Lara," he said hoarsely against her neck, "I need—"

"—to hurry up," she interrupted. "Please, hurry."

Graeme ditched his good intentions. Her voice

trembled with urgency, and there was no way he could refuse her. He couldn't remember the last time he'd been this aroused. Okay, that wasn't strictly true; he'd been pretty damned hot for Lara just a while ago in his penthouse suite. But aside from Lara, he couldn't think of another woman who turned him on so completely. He felt desperate and his fingers trembled as he cradled the fragile line of her jaw in his hands. He searched her eyes and saw the same need reflected there before he angled her face for his kiss.

She moaned softly against his lips. Her mouth was soft, but her tongue slid strongly against his even as she pushed her free hand beneath the hem of his shirt and over his skin. She sucked on his tongue, drawing a hoarse moan of pleasure from him. He cradled her scalp in one hand, and covered her breast with his other, reveling in the lush fullness.

Lara dragged her lips free, breathing heavily. "I have to see you," she said huskily, and pushed his shirt up over his chest. Graeme helped her, pulling it over his head and tossing it onto the floor.

Her hands were everywhere, sliding over his pecs to his shoulders, and down the length of his ribs to his abdomen, and then lower, to where his jeans were unfastened.

"You're so beautiful," she breathed, pressing her mouth against his chest. "Even more beautiful than I remembered."

"You've got it all wrong, love," he rumbled, dragging her T-shirt up over her head and tossing it onto the floor near his own. "You're the beautiful one." He cupped her breasts, lifting them and circling the dusky nipples with his thumbs. "So pretty," he murmured, before bending his head to flick his tongue against one distended tip.

Lara gasped softly and her hands moved to his head, her fingers tunneling through his hair as she hummed her approval.

"Take these off," she demanded, and Graeme swiftly complied, kicking off his sandals and shucking his jeans. Lara leaned back a little and her eyes darkened to cobalt as she devoured the sight of him.

"Oh," she murmured, and her hand closed around his jutting erection. "You're so gorgeous."

Graeme couldn't help but laugh a little, but the sincerity in her voice caused him to swell even more. "And you're wearing too many clothes," he replied gruffly, grasping her by the hips and pulling her closer. "These need to come off."

He helped her strip out of the panties, bending to slide the scrap of lace down the length of her legs. When, finally, she wore nothing, Graeme's mouth went dry. He hadn't thought anything could be as erotic as her slave-girl costume, but he'd been wrong. Seeing her standing in front of him, looking simultaneously shy and sexy, exceeded all the fantasies he'd had of her, and he'd had plenty.

He didn't have time to stand back and admire her, though, because as soon as he straightened she launched herself at him, sliding her arms around him as she pressed her body against his.

"The way you look at me makes me feel all hot and quivery inside," she said against his skin. "I like it."

Graeme smiled and smoothed his hands over her back to the silken curve of her buttocks, pulling her flush against his body. He couldn't explain the way he felt, and wasn't sure he wanted to. Holding Lara felt right, but beneath that he was aware of an aching sensation that began deep in his chest and blossomed outward.

She wanted a divorce.

He would give it to her, of course. He'd made a promise to her father that if she came to him and asked him to release her from the marriage, then he would do it. Right now, however, he didn't want to think about letting her go. Didn't want to think about her with any other man. For the moment, at least, she was his.

"You feel so good." She sighed in pleasure, rubbing herself against him like a sensual cat. "I want to touch you everywhere."

As if to prove her words, she slid her hands down to stroke his back, before moving lower. Graeme couldn't prevent a small growl of satisfaction when she cupped his buttocks and pulled him closer. For just an instant they stared at each other. Graeme saw the need and promise in her eyes, and with a groan of surrender, he bent his head and fastened his mouth over hers. Her lips opened beneath his and her tongue slid against his own. A fresh wave of desire swamped his brain and traveled down his spine like an electric current, shutting down any ability to think rationally.

With an urgency he couldn't control, he smoothed his palms over the slender curve of her back to cup her buttocks. She moaned into his mouth and squirmed against him as her hands clutched his back. Graeme could feel her heat pressed against him, and the scent of her desire wafted over him until he felt dizzy with the force of his lust. He'd forgotten how good she smelled. He could easily become intoxicated on the taste of her.

With a small grunt, Graeme lifted her up, gratified when she hooked her legs around his hips. She wound her arms tightly around his neck and speared her tongue against his, making small noises of approval in the back of her throat. Her fingers dug into the muscles of his back, but Graeme hardly noticed.

He turned with her in his arms, still holding her luscious rear in his hands, until her back was pressed against the nearest wall. His cock was right there, pressed against her center, and it took no more than one powerful thrust to bury himself in her slick heat.

Lara cried out softly, and then used her thighs to leverage herself up and down on his shaft. Graeme thought he'd never felt anything as amazing as the sensation of Lara's body fisted tightly around his own. She weighed nothing, and it was no effort at all to support her in his hands as he angled his hips upward, each thrust driving him closer to release.

But he wasn't ready to end their lovemaking so soon. He wanted to make it last, because once they were through they were…well, through.

Lara wound her arms tighter around his shoulders and her breath came in quick, warm pants against his neck. "Please, please," she gasped.

"Ah, damn," he groaned. "This feels too good. Here, let's do this."

He turned without withdrawing from her body and in one stride, reached the enormous bed. He eased Lara onto the mattress, gritting his teeth against the sensation of pulling free from her heat. She refused to release him entirely, hooking her hands behind his neck and pulling him down beside her.

"Don't leave."

"I had no intention, love," he said grimly, and shifted her so that he could lie alongside her. "There's something I want to do."

Lara twisted to look directly at him, her eyes still hazy with sexual pleasure. "Anything you want," she said, smiling as she read the intent in his expression.

Graeme slid one arm beneath her shoulders, pulling her into a more comfortable position against his chest. He tipped her face up and lowered his mouth back to hers, feasting on her lush lips and using his tongue to tease her until she shifted restlessly against him.

He smoothed his free hand down the length of her body, palming her soft breasts and teasing her nipples until she moaned into his mouth and pushed her hips against his. Graeme knew what she wanted, and he slid his hand over her stomach until he reached the apex of her thighs, urging them apart. He parted her damp curls until he found her center, and swirled his finger over the slick little nub nestled there.

"Oh," Lara gasped, and her thighs fell open to grant him better access.

Graeme smiled against her lips, absorbing her small noises of pleasure. Her arousal thrilled him, made him feel as if he was king of the world because he was the one who doing this to her, making her crazy with need. He increased his movements until she trembled and pushed her hips against his hand. When he eased a finger into her, she gave a soft cry, and arched toward him, sliding her thigh over his hip as she strained for more of the intimate contact.

She was wet and swollen with desire, and Graeme carefully inserted a second finger, stretching her to accommodate him, and used the pad of his thumb to torment the small rise of flesh.

"Oh, Graeme," she said brokenly.

"I'm here, love," he said, his voice roughened with emotion. He used his tongue to open her mouth, sweeping inside even as he increased the movement of his fingers. Lara trembled, and her hands clutched at him convulsively.

"Omigod," she gasped, dragging her mouth to stare up at him with something like amazement. Her lips were parted and swollen from his kisses, her eyes heavy-lidded and dazed with arousal. "I'm going to come."

Graeme's body responded to her words, his cock so heavy and aching that it took all his restraint not to push her legs apart and sink into her slick heat. But he wanted this to be about her pleasure; he wanted to make her happy, even if it was just for a short time. He wanted to memorize how she looked, wanted to lock this moment into his brain so that he could replay it in minute detail later on. So he swallowed thickly and watched in utter fascination as she stiffened in his arms and then shuddered, her entire body flushed with her building orgasm.

Her eyes locked with his as her inner muscles contracted around his fingers and her hips bucked, and a harsh cry was torn from her throat, until finally she went limp and her head dropped back to the mattress, her breathing ragged.

"Oh," she finally breathed, "that was…incredible."

Graeme tightened his arm around her and pressed

his lips against her temple. Watching her *had* been amazing. He didn't think he'd ever tire of seeing her come undone with him.

Unbidden, an image of her doing this with another man filled his head. Jealousy, fierce and hard and hot, swamped him. He rolled onto his back beside Lara and flung an arm over his eyes, as if by doing so he could block out the mental pictures that played through his mind.

He felt the mattress dip as Lara raised herself on one elbow and looked down at him. When she cupped his jaw with one hand, he cracked an eyelid to look at her. Her face was flushed, her damp hair beginning to dry in wild disarray around her face. Her eyes were clouded now, watching him with a mixture of trepidation and concern.

"Are you okay?" she asked, and caught her lower lip between her teeth, nibbling on the fullness.

Graeme groaned and reaching up, buried his hands in her hair and drew her down for a kiss that seemed to reach into his very soul. When they finally pulled apart, they were both breathing hard. Lara's hair curtained their faces as she traced a finger along his lower lip.

"You always were a good kisser," she murmured reflectively.

"You always made it easy for me," Graeme said huskily, fastening his gaze on her lips. "Your mouth drives me mad."

He watched, entranced, as her face and neck blushed with color. Leaning forward, she gave him a soft, moist, openmouthed kiss that ricocheted straight to his groin and caused him to swell even more.

"My mouth is going to drive you mad," she promised,

and before Graeme could guess her intent, she began working her way down the length of his body, stroking him with her hands as she covered his bare skin with hot, wet kisses.

He bent his arms behind his head to watch her, knowing more than just her mouth drove him crazy. In fact, he was beginning to suspect that he was falling hard for his own wife.

LARA'S BODY still thrummed with the remnants of the powerful orgasm she'd had, but having Graeme's body beneath her hands made her want more. She wanted to absorb him, to pull him into her body until she couldn't tell where he ended and she began.

His skin was like hot silk beneath her lips as she worked her way down the length of his body. She felt like a supplicant, smoothing her hands along the underside of his arms and reveling in the bulge of his biceps, before skimming lower, along the fingered muscles of his ribs to his stomach. She heard his breath hiss in sharply when she reached his straining penis, and she grasped it lightly in her hands. It throbbed strongly against her palm.

Lara knelt between Graeme's legs and devoured the sight of him. His shaft was darkly flushed and thick, straining toward her. Lara held him in one hand and slowly circled the pad of her finger over the curved cap, teasing the tiny slit and coaxing a dewy drop of moisture from him.

Graeme groaned, and Lara glanced up at him. Twin patches of color rode high on his cheekbones as he watched her through half-closed lids. With his arms bent behind his head, he looked supremely male. Lara swallowed thickly at the thought of having him inside her, of stroking him intimately with her body. Despite their encounter in his room, she felt suddenly shy. Only the heat she saw in Graeme's eyes made her feel bold enough to continue.

"Do you want me to do this?" she asked softly, and keeping her eyes on Graeme's face, she tasted him delicately with her tongue.

His jaw clenched and his muscles went rigid, but his voice was low and sexy. "Do whatever makes you happy, love. You'll hear no complaints from me."

"This makes me happy," Lara assured him, and dipping her head, she traced her tongue along the contours of his shaft. He tasted clean and sweet, his skin warm and pulsing beneath her tongue. Gripping the base of his cock with one hand, Lara cupped his balls and gently massaged them as she slowly drew him into her mouth, sliding her tongue along his length.

Graeme made a guttural noise deep in his throat and, as if he couldn't help himself, his hips came up off the bed. His increased arousal made Lara squirm with her own building excitement. She increased her efforts, taking as much of his length into her mouth as she could and then letting him slide almost completely free before drawing him in again.

Reaching down, he buried one hand in her hair, his fingers massaging her scalp and urging her on. Glancing up at him, she saw his face was flushed, his expression one of tight concentration as he watched her.

"Suck me, love," he whispered hoarsely.

Lara did, drawing hard on him and tasting his essence on her tongue. She knew he was close, and although she'd never experienced a man's release in her mouth before, there was no way she was going to stop.

With a harsh groan, Graeme pulled himself free from her mouth, his breathing labored. "Not like this," he panted, and catching Lara's arms, he hauled upward until she lay sprawled on top of him.

He kissed her deeply, his tongue tangling with hers as his hands kneaded her bottom and he ground himself against her pelvis. Lara knew she was wet, so aroused by what she'd done that she could feel herself pulsing with need.

"Come inside me, Graeme," she whispered. "I'm so…"

She couldn't finish the sentence, but she didn't need to. Graeme sat up, cupping her face in his hands and kissing her one last time. "Turn around," he commanded softly.

"What?"

With Graeme's hands guiding her, Lara found herself on her knees, facing away from him. He knelt behind her, his big hands smoothing over her bottom. Knowing he had a full view of her most private parts made Lara feel both self-conscious and incredibly sexy at the same time. She looked back at him over her shoulder. His gaze was fixed on her bottom, and the expression on his face was so purely male that Lara felt herself weep with moisture.

"Do you want me like this?" she asked, and lowered her elbows to the mattress and arched her back in invitation.

"Oh, aye," he groaned. "If you could see what I see…"

But Lara's eyes were fixed on Graeme. His erection jutted strongly from his body, and she didn't want to wait any longer for him to fill her. To love her.

"Please, Graeme," she begged.

"Ah, damn," he said, and Laura saw him take himself in his hand, then felt him nudge the entrance to her body. He moved with aching slowness, rubbing himself along her cleft until Lara thought she might lose it right then and there.

"Hurry, hurry," she panted, but his control was amazing.

"I want this to last," he muttered, and held her hips still with one hand, preventing her from thrusting backward. Lara thought she might die from wanting him. But then he eased forward, filling her with excruciating slowness, stretching her in a way she'd never experienced before. The sensation was indescribable as her body accepted him, but still he held her immobile, not permitting her to take more of him than he was willing to give.

"Graeme!" she pleaded. "I need to move."

Graeme came over her then, covering her with his body and sweeping her hair to one side so that he could kiss her neck and nip lightly at her earlobe, his breathing harsh. Lara pushed back against him, loving the feel of him as he thrust strongly inside her. Bracing himself on one hand, he used his free hand to fondle her breasts, lightly rolling and pinching her nipples until Lara heard herself moaning in pleasure.

"That's it, love." His voice was ragged. "Come for me."

His hand slid across her stomach and delved between her legs, until he found the slick nub of her clitoris and swirled his finger over it in delicious torment.

Lara was so close, every cell in her body straining

for release, the liquid heat of her body pulsing with demand. She twisted her face and Graeme kissed her, even as he angled his hips and thrust once, then twice, and his body jerked with his powerful release as a groan was ripped from his throat.

The combination was too much for Lara, and she convulsed around him as her orgasm shimmered through her, joining him in utter and complete bliss.

10

GRAEME LAY BACK against the pillows with Lara curled warmly against him. Her hair spread over his shoulder like a skein of red-gold silk, and she lazily traced one finger across his chest. He tipped her face up and studied her flushed features. "I guess some things never change."

It was no more than the truth. Whenever he was around Lara, his ability to think rationally or make educated decisions went out the window. He still couldn't believe they'd just had sex without the benefit of protection. He'd been so overcome with the need to have her that he hadn't even thought of a condom. Not that it would have mattered; he hadn't brought any protection with him. He'd been so furious with the way she'd bolted from his room earlier that his only thought had been to confront her and demand to know what she wanted from him.

He gave a huff of wry laughter. She'd pretty much answered that question for him—a quick divorce and some really hot sex, and not necessarily in that order. Did she even realize what they'd just done? He wasn't worried about disease; he was clean and he'd stake his life on the fact that Lara was, too. But he had no clue if she was on the pill, or if she used any other kind of protection. Christ, he could have gotten her pregnant.

Oddly, the thought of Lara having his child didn't terrify him quite as much as it should have. With any other woman, he might have felt differently, but then he'd never forgotten to use protection with any other women. He had no memories of his own father, who had left when he was just a toddler. He'd sworn he'd never get a woman pregnant unless he was willing to make a lifetime commitment to her and the child. As a result, he'd always been scrupulously careful. It was the one aspect of sex that he'd been unwilling to make compromises about.

But where Lara was concerned, he'd never been able to say no. When he'd let her talk him into eloping to Scotland, all his arguments that she should return to the States and finish her degree before settling down had been brushed aside. He simply couldn't say no to her. Not then. Not now.

"You say some things never change like it's a bad thing," Lara murmured, bringing him out of his reverie. She slid a leg across his, rubbing herself sensuously against him like a small, contented cat.

Graeme gritted his teeth against the sensation of her silken limbs against his skin. What they'd shared *had* been incredible, and it scared the hell out of him because it made him realize that he hadn't come close to getting over her.

While everything in him wanted to gather her into his arms and reassure her that they had a future together, he'd been down that road before. He'd told her the truth when he'd said that he had no control where she was concerned. All it took was one kiss, one heated look from her sapphire eyes, and he was complete putty in her hands.

Five years ago, he'd given her everything he had—his heart and his name—and she'd left him with nothing but the bitter taste of betrayal in his mouth. But from the instant he'd laid eyes on her in the ballroom, he'd known he was in trouble. It would take so little for him to fall back under her spell, and the kicker was that she didn't even realize the power she had over him. If she so much as crooked her little finger in his direction, he'd be her willing slave.

He had no idea what it meant, but he rejected any notion that he was still in love with her. She'd annihilated any tender feelings he might have had the day she climbed into her daddy's limousine and drove out of his life. The best explanation he could come up with was that he enjoyed having sex with her. Okay, he more than enjoyed it. He absolutely couldn't get enough of her, but was damned if he could figure out why.

He'd desired other women, but never with the same fierce need and intensity that accompanied his desire for Lara. He'd never had a problem walking away from women before. In fact, once he'd had sex with a woman, he typically lost interest in her. With Lara, however, he no sooner had one mind-blowing orgasm with her than his devious mind began crafting ways in which he might have another.

"Lara, listen to me," he said softly, raising himself on one elbow so that he could look at her face. She gazed up at him with so much trust and warmth in her eyes that he felt his insides tighten. Reaching out, he caught a tendril of hair that was stuck to the corner of her mouth and freed it, smoothing it back from her face.

"What is it?"

He lifted her hand from his chest and turned it over in his, stroking his thumb across her palm. He kept his eyes focused on their hands, sharply aware of her nudity. Lust coiled in his groin, and, even after the amazing orgasm he'd just had, he could feel his body respond to her nearness. It would be easy to lose himself in her, to spend the next several hours, or even days, exploring each other. But he needed to stay focused.

"We need to talk about what just happened."

She smiled in contentment. "Mmm. It was perfect."

Graeme frowned, frustrated. "Is that what you're going to tell your boyfriend? That you came to Las Vegas and had perfect sex with your soon-to-be ex-husband?" He couldn't keep the bitterness out of his voice. "That ought to go over well."

Lara's eyes widened, and in that instant Graeme realized she'd completely forgotten about her boyfriend. Had forgotten she even had a boyfriend. He was pretty sure that for the past hour, she'd even forgotten that she wanted a divorce.

Horror slowly replaced the expression of sensual satisfaction in her blue eyes, and she pulled her hand free from his and sat up, crossing her arms over her breasts as if only now aware of her nudity.

"Oh my God," she breathed, staring at him in distress. "What have I done?" She leaped from the bed, searching for her underwear and T-shirt amongst the clothing scattered on the floor.

Graeme watched her. "I'd say you just had sex with your husband," he drawled.

She jerked upright, holding his T-shirt against her breasts. "Husband? Technically, maybe, but we haven't even seen each other in five years. Up until tonight, you were a husband in name only." She shook her head as she bent over and picked up his jeans, searching beneath them. "I can't believe this. I'm with you for less than five minutes and I fall all over you like a sex-crazed lunatic." She snatched her underwear off the floor and turned to pinion him with an accusing glare. "This is all your fault, you know."

Graeme didn't bother to deny her words. He sat up and swung his legs over the side of the bed, his eyes traveling over her in slow appreciation. "Why is it all my fault? I don't recall you protesting."

Her brows knitted in a frown as she looked at him. "Because you're so—you're so damned *you,* that's why!" With a groan of sheer frustration, she flung her panties at him, striking him directly in the center of his chest. "There. Now you even have me throwing my underwear at you. Happy? I'm so pathetic."

Graeme flung the scrap of lace onto the bed and stood up. She looked so miserable that he felt his heart twist. He tipped her chin up, forcing her to look at him. To his dismay, tears shimmered in her eyes.

"Lara, you're crying." He cupped her face in his hands. "Does this other bloke mean so much, then?" He asked the question, but he didn't know if he was ready to hear her answer.

"Yes." She sniffed. "No. Oh, I don't know. Christopher is a really nice guy, and he treats me well."

Even though Graeme had just slept with the "really nice guy's" girlfriend, he resented the hell out of the other man. Resented him because Lara liked him and spent time with him.

"He's a nice guy and he treats you well?" he repeated sarcastically. "Sounds like a basis for a solid, lasting relationship."

"Yes, well, I thought so, too." Lara jerked her face away from his fingers. "At least until I found out that you and I— That we were—"

"Still married," Graeme supplied.

"Yes."

Graeme bent and retrieved his jeans, jerking them on with rough movements. "So you came to ask me for a divorce so you could marry this nice guy who treats you well." He snorted. "Because I'm such an asshole and I treated you so poorly."

Lara glared at him before pulling his T-shirt on over her head. The hem came down to her thighs, and Graeme wondered if she knew how completely sexy and alluring she looked, with her hair tousled and her skin still flushed from his lovemaking. Had Christopher seen her like this? The mere thought made him want to pummel the other man into oblivion.

Lara pushed her hair back from her face. "If it makes you feel any better, I never blamed you for treating me poorly. I'm sure it came as a huge shock to find out I wasn't the girl you thought I was."

Memories of that horrible day in Scotland came flooding back. "You think I treated you poorly, Lara? After your dad came bursting into our room and literally snatched you out of my bed, and then proceeded to tell me that you'd lied to me? That you were no more than a bairn out of the schoolroom?" He laughed in disbelief and raked a hand over his hair. "I wanted to strangle you for botching things so royally. For not trusting me with the truth." He grabbed her by the upper arms and hauled her close, until their faces were no more than an inch apart. "I'd have waited for you, Lara, I loved you that much. You didn't need to lie to me."

"You wouldn't even look at me," she whispered. "When my father told you that I was only seventeen, you looked at me once and then refused to meet my eyes again."

He shook her lightly. "Jesus, Lara, I'd just spent two days debauching a *teenager!* When I think of the things I did to you…I felt like I'd ruined you. Like I'd taken something clean and pure and sullied it."

"But I loved you. I loved what we did together," Lara said earnestly. "I was going to turn eighteen in just two weeks. The other girls in my school had been doing those things since they were sixteen. I didn't feel sullied. I felt sexy and loved."

Graeme groaned, closing his eyes briefly against the memories. "You *were* sexy." *And loved.* Letting Lara go had been the hardest thing he'd ever done, hands-down, but he wasn't about to tell her that. She already had too much control over him.

"I waited for you."

Graeme opened his eyes and stared down at Lara. He saw the pain she'd felt reflected in her eyes and he wanted to tell her that he had come for her; he'd followed her to the States. But he'd also have to tell her how her father had ensured he wouldn't gain entry.

His visa had been denied and there was no question in Graeme's mind that Lara's father was responsible. But whatever Brent Whitfield had done to him, he was still Lara's father and Graeme wouldn't be responsible for diminishing him in her eyes. He'd paid a lot of legal fees to have his record cleared, but it had been more than two years before he'd finally been issued a new visa. By then, Lara had been a junior in college and had seemed to be happy with her life.

"I'm sorry," he said simply. "I figured you'd moved on with your life."

She stared at him, and Graeme felt about two inches tall when he saw the disappointment and hurt on her face. "Actually, that's why I came here," she finally said, drawing in a deep breath and visibly pulling herself together. "To put you behind me so that I *could* finally move on with my life."

He put up a hand to forestall her. "I know…with Christopher, the nice guy who treats you well. Is it working?"

Lara didn't pretend to misunderstand him. "No," she said, sounding miserable.

Graeme's mood shifted, and he suddenly felt lighter than he had in a long time. "So what's the problem? You've seen me. Christ, you've had me in every way possible. What more do you want?"

One of the things he'd always loved about Lara was her candor, and her inability to hide her feelings from him. Now she looked at him, her expression glum. "If you must know the truth, I deliberately seduced you earlier tonight."

"Ah."

Lara began pacing the small room. "As soon as I realized you didn't recognize me, I planned this whole scenario of seduction, thinking you'd never know it was me."

As if.

Graeme leaned negligently against the bedpost and watched her, trying to keep the smug satisfaction he felt from showing on his face. Lara kept talking, her hands moving in concert with her lips. The words tumbled from her mouth heedlessly, helplessly, as if she was compelled to tell him the truth.

"I had this crazy idea that if I could just have you again, that maybe I could finally get you out of my system. But instead, I just want more of you—isn't that insane? I mean, I know it's only because my body has been deprived for so long. And you're *Graeme Hamilton!* The sexiest man alive. I mean, any woman would want you, right?"

Graeme stilled and then eased himself away from the bedpost. His tone was tight, every muscle in his body taut. "What are you saying, love? That Christopher is too *nice* to take you to his bed?"

Lara stopped and stared at him, color flooding her cheeks. "We don't have that kind of relationship," she mumbled.

"Then why the hell are you with the bloke?" Graeme's voice was low.

Lara tipped her chin up, her expression mutinous. "Because he *is* a nice guy, and because he *does* treat me well. He'll give me all the things I want and need."

"Things that I can't, I suppose?" Graeme's earlier lightness had tightened into a hard knot.

"Not with your lifestyle," she argued. "You're always moving from location to location, depending on where your latest project is being shot. When you're not filming, you're attending premieres or other red-carpet events. You have a demanding schedule, Graeme. Just look at all the interviews that your publicist is trying to set up for you, not just here in the States, but around the world." She looked helplessly at him. "How could that possibly be conducive to settling down and raising a family?"

"Other celebrities seem to manage it just fine," he said tightly. "Look at Tom Hanks or Denzel Washington. But if that's really how you feel, then you'd best hope our little oversight just now doesn't result in a pregnancy. Because if you are pregnant, there'll be no divorce and I *will* be there to raise my child."

Lara stared at him in bewilderment for a moment, and then realization washed over her. One hand flew to her mouth even as the other one fluttered to her stomach. "We forgot to use protection."

"Aye."

They stared at each other for a long moment. Lara broke the contact first. Graeme watched with regret as she found her panties and slipped them on, pulling them into place.

"So now what do we do?" she asked.

Graeme stepped past Lara and moved to the bedside table. Lifting the bulky envelope that contained her costume, he tossed it onto the upholstered chair nearby. He picked up the silver locket, letting it dangle from the end of his finger.

"If you're so anxious to move on with your life, why have you kept this all these years?"

Lara chewed her lip. "I never said I'd stopped thinking about you," she finally answered. "Only that I want to. I realized after my father died that I'd been living in a fantasy world, believing you might eventually come for me." She gave a huff of bitter laughter. "Obviously that didn't happen. I decided I needed to put you in my past, to get over you once and for all." She twisted her fingers together. "I thought if I slept with you again, then I'd realize that you weren't nearly as good as I'd remembered and that I could finally move on."

Graeme caught the locket in his palm and closed his hand around it. He stepped closer to her. "And was I? As good as you remembered?"

Lara closed her eyes briefly. When she opened them, Graeme could see the conflict there. "No," she finally answered. "You were better."

11

"I HAVE a proposition for you."

Lara looked up from the French toast with brandied bananas and pecans that she'd been toying with, and eyed Graeme warily.

It was early morning, and they were sitting at a corner table of the lavish hotel restaurant, overlooking a lush veranda and the hotel pool. Graeme had suggested they come down to the restaurant for breakfast before his interview with the local television station. He wanted to break the news to Tony Angelini about their marriage.

The one thing Lara had nearly forgotten about Graeme was how much he enjoyed good food. On their first real date in London, Graeme had taken her to a jazz club located in a Regency townhouse near Buckingham Palace. The club had a distinctly Scottish flavor, with dining rooms that had names like the Jacobite Room and McGregor's Bar. Lara had understood that he was proud of his Scottish heritage and had wanted to share something of Scotland with her.

The establishment had been decorated in the style of a classic gentleman's club, with rich red walls hung with oil paintings and ornate mirrors, the dark, polished woodwork gleaming softly beneath gas lights, and linen-covered tables set with tiny candles. She and Graeme had shared a meal of wild salmon, minted carrots and mashed potatoes. He had explained to her that Scotland was famous for its salmon, and that his grandfather had sometimes taken him and his brother fishing when they were small. Lara had gotten the sense that Graeme hadn't had much growing up, and so found appreciation in the simplest of things, like wild salmon, cooked to perfection.

They'd finished their dinner with a snifter of single-malt Macallan whiskey that had both warmed Lara from the inside and loosened her limbs. Even then, Lara knew the evening must have cost Graeme more money than he could really afford, but he'd seemed to derive a great deal of pleasure from Lara's enjoyment of the experience.

Now she watched as Graeme finished his breakfast of eggs, corned beef and pastrami hash, crispy potatoes and smoked herring. Lara had been reluctant to leave the hotel room, and even more hesitant to be seen in public with Graeme, but the Mediterranean-style restaurant was almost empty at this early hour.

"What kind of proposition?" she asked, watching him carefully. His jaw was shadowed with a day's growth of beard, and his eyes reflected weariness from lack of sleep. Lara thought he'd never looked so sexy or appealing and for a moment she glimpsed a stark vulnerability in his eyes that caused her breath to catch in her throat.

"I think we'd both agree that there's something here. Some kind of chemistry between us."

Lara looked pointedly behind him, where a waitress laid place settings on tables. She smiled politely at

Graeme when he glanced over at her, and continued with her task.

"Maybe you were right. Maybe coming down here wasn't such a good idea," he muttered.

"I don't think she overheard us. Aside from her, there's really nobody else here," Lara said, looking around. It was early enough that except for an older couple on the other side of the dining room, the restaurant was empty. "Go on with your...proposition. I agree that there is definitely a chemistry, if you want to call it that."

He shrugged. "Whatever it is, I think it's worth exploring a bit, don't you?"

"What do you mean?"

He blew out a hard breath. "I mean that before we make any decisions about the future, we should figure out what this...thing is between us."

"It's lust, Graeme, plain and simple."

"Well, if you're right about that, then we should be able to work it out of our systems, right?"

Lara brushed a hand over her eyes. "I can't believe we're even having this conversation."

Graeme dipped his head to look directly into her eyes. "But that's just what you were hoping to do when you came to my room last night, right? You thought by having sex with me that you'd finally get me out of your system. Then you'd divorce me, settle down with Mr. Nice and raise a houseful of babies with no regrets. Am I right?"

Lara lowered her hand and looked at him. "Yes."

"Lara, I have to tell you that it's been a long time since I've wanted a woman as much as I want you." He raised a hand to forestall her words. "I can't afford to be getting into a long relationship. That's not what I'm looking for. Truthfully, I'd already planned on asking you for a divorce before I left for New Zealand next month."

Lara stopped breathing. Her stomach did an alarming flip and she tried desperately to ignore the hammering of her heart against her ribs. He hadn't wanted her after all! He'd been planning on ending their marriage. The knowledge came as a painful blow, despite the fact that she had been seeking the same thing of him.

"I see. So then, I guess there's no point in delaying the inevitable." Her hand went to her pocketbook, where she had stashed the sheaf of legal documents. She hadn't wanted to leave them in the room where a housekeeper might see them. "I brought the papers with me," she said dully. "If you'd like, we can sign them now and be done with this whole thing."

"Wait."

Was that amusement she heard lacing his voice?

Reluctantly, she raised her eyes to his. A small smile played around his mouth.

"You haven't heard my proposition, yet."

Lara raised her eyebrows, waiting. She couldn't imagine what he might have in mind, and wasn't sure she wanted any part of it, anyway. "Is it legal?"

"Oh, aye, at least until we sign those papers." Pushing his plate aside, he leaned across the table toward her. "Do you remember the inn where we spent our wedding night?"

Lara drew in a deep breath, recalling the secluded Scottish hideaway, and the charmingly romantic room where they'd spent two nights together. If she closed her eyes, she could even see the four-poster bed with the plaid coverlet, the little grate where Graeme had lit a fire for them, and the tiny washroom where he'd folded his long frame into the tub and pulled her in to share a bath with him.

"Yes," she said quietly. "I remember. It was called the Kirkhouse Inn."

Graeme drew in a deep breath. "Okay, here's the proposition. We're legally married, and you said yourself that you're not sleeping with that bloke."

"His name is Christopher." Lara gave him a pointed look. "I'm not sleeping with Christopher *yet*."

"Right." Reaching over, he laced his fingers with hers. "So before we dissolve the marriage, and before we both move on with our bright and happy futures, I propose we spend two days—just two days—at the inn. Together."

Whatever she'd expected Graeme to say, he hadn't even come close. Lara gaped at him and tried desperately not to let him see how tempting his proposition sounded.

"And the point would be…?"

Graeme grinned unabashedly. "To have as much sex as we possibly can."

The sound of crashing silverware startled them both, and they looked over to where the waitress had upset a bin of utensils that she carried. She gave them an apologetic smile as she hurriedly scooped the silverware back into the bin.

Lara returned her attention to Graeme. "I'm still not getting it, Graeme."

He waggled his eyebrows at her. "Come with me and you will, love. I guarantee it."

The way he rolled his *R*s made Lara shiver deliciously. She told herself that it was only his persuasive Scots tongue that had her thinking seriously about his proposition, and not because she had a hankering for more sex. With him.

Still, she had to be certain she understood exactly what he was suggesting. She pulled her hands free. "You want to return to the inn in Scotland and spend two nights there, having sex?"

"Two days and two nights," he clarified. "And I'm actually kidding about the sex, although I'll do whatever will make you happy and if that includes sacrificing my body to your appetites, then so be it." He saw her dismayed expression and held up his hands. "I'm kidding. Really. My thought was actually to go somewhere quiet, away from this circus. The inn is off the beaten path and trust me when I say that nobody there will care who I am." He laughed. "Funny thing about Scotland—it's the one place I can go where nobody recognizes me."

Lara stared at him, bemused. "But why go back to the inn? We could go anywhere."

Graeme actually looked embarrassed as he shrugged. "I think we both have a lot of memories wrapped up in that inn. We were so young." He linked his fingers together, letting his hands rest on the tablecloth. "Sometimes I wonder if we were more in love with the idea of love itself than we were with each other. Does that make sense?" He glanced up at Lara, his expression taut.

Lara swallowed thickly. He was implying that they had never actually been in love. Not truly in love. She wanted to reject the very thought, because if that was true then she had spent the last five years of her life yearning for an illusion, a fantasy.

"I don't think that's the case," she said, mortified to hear the wobble in her voice.

Reaching over, Graeme caught her hands in his. He stroked them between his own, as if she were chilled and he could restore warmth to her hands. "I'm not saying that's the case, I'm just saying it's a possibility. But I think we need to go back there and take another look at those days. We've both done a lot of growing up and I think we'll see that our memories are idealized."

"You don't think those two days and nights that we spent together were as good as we both remember them being?"

Graeme blew out a hard breath. "I don't know. There's no question that we have great chemistry, but has it ever been anything more than that? I just don't know, Lara." He dipped his head to look into her face. "Come with me to Scotland. Just for a few days. We won't make any decisions until then, okay? But I think we need to get out of this environment. As long as we're here, you're only going to think of me as Graeme the actor. As Kip Corrigan."

"That's not true," she protested.

"It is. I can hardly blame you for thinking of me like that." He gave a rueful grin. "Not when every person in this hotel thinks of me as Kip. That's why we need to be alone, where nobody recognizes me or cares who I am. Where I can just be myself and not worry about the damned photographers or reporters stalking my every move."

"But you're leaving for New Zealand. That's not going to change."

"No, that won't change. But I'm not leaving until next month. We have time to figure this thing out."

Lara's heart began to beat fast. She felt confused and more than a little scared by the prospect. She didn't know if she could be with Graeme for two days, not if there was a possibility that he would walk away from her in the end. It was one thing to be the person asking for a divorce; it was another thing altogether to be the one left behind.

"I don't know, Graeme…"

"It's a brilliant plan, Lara. I think we'll both realize that our memories of those two nights and each other have been so exaggerated and so built up in our minds, that for the past five years no other person has been able to live up to our expectations."

Lara glanced sharply at Graeme, but he wasn't looking at her. He was staring fixedly at their linked hands, as if they held some secret that he would ferret out.

Had Graeme built her up in his mind over the past five years? Had other women paled in comparison to her? She fervently hoped so.

"Do you think two days will be enough time?" she asked doubtfully.

For herself, she couldn't imagine that a couple of days would be sufficient time for her to figure out the complex jumble of emotions she felt for Graeme. She knew it wouldn't be enough time for her to grow physically bored with him. Although, in retrospect, she'd been so done with the coconut-covered marshmallows after just a few hours of gorging herself on them. And at nine years old, she'd been convinced that she could live the rest of her life on nothing but those sweet confections.

Graeme raised his head. "I don't know. But let's start with two days. If after that time you're ready for me to sign the divorce papers, then I'll sign them."

Lara hesitated. There was a catch in there some-where, but for the life of her, she couldn't figure out what it was.

"And what if you've had enough of me after two days?" she asked. "What if I want more time, but you don't?" She drew in a deep breath. "What if I decide that I really am in love with you, but you don't feel the same way? What if you decide that you just want to be single again?"

From nearby came the clatter of dishware and both Lara and Graeme turned to see the waitress scrambling to straighten a small stack of cups and saucers at the nearby waitress station. This time she didn't look over at them, but picked up a pot of coffee and walked toward the elderly couple on the other side of the res-taurant.

"Let's cross that bridge when and if we come to it," Graeme suggested.

He gave Lara a smile that caused her heart to turn over, and alarm bells went off somewhere in her head. She recognized the danger signs; she was already half-way to falling in love with him all over again.

"What am I going to tell Christopher?"

Lara wasn't aware that she'd spoken aloud until Graeme answered. His eyes gleamed with an unholy light. "Personally, I think you should tell him you're going to Scotland to fuck me blind."

"YOU'RE GOING to do *what?*"

Lara cringed at the sheer disbelief in Val's voice.

"It makes perfect sense, Val," she argued, frowning at the cell phone. She'd put it on speaker-phone mode and placed it on the bed while she hastily repacked her suitcase, stuffing her clothing haphazardly inside. "I mean, do I really want to get into a serious relationship with Christopher if I have doubts?"

"Forget about Christopher for a moment," Val said, exasperated. "What do you think you're going to prove by going to Scotland with Graeme? Don't you see what he's up to?"

"What?"

"He's just using you, Lara! I mean, c'mon—the guy hasn't so much as sent you a postcard in the last five years, and now suddenly the two of you need to spend the next couple of days locked together in a hotel room?" She made a scoffing sound. "You're not really going to fall for that, are you?"

"He's not using me, Val. At least not any more than I'm using him. I only know that if I don't do this, I'll always regret it. Don't you understand? I've gone through the last five years wondering what might have been. Now I have a chance to see if all that angst and longing was based in reality, or if it was just a figment of my own overactive imagination."

"Yeah, right." Valerie sound skeptical. "Or you're just looking for new material for your writing. After all, you only spent two nights with him and that was five years ago. I mean, c'mon, how many stories can you create from two measly nights?"

Lara recalled those two nights and shivered. Some of her hottest stories had been based on those two measly nights. Even Val didn't know the extent of what she and Graeme had shared during their time together at the inn.

"I'm not looking for new material," she said patiently, although she silently acknowledged that the past night had given her all kinds of new material, if she chose to continue writing. "I'm trying to find out if there really is something between us. Maybe Graeme Hamilton is a complete jerk, and once I'm no longer lusting over his body, I'll see him for what he really is."

"Uh-huh. Sure." Valerie's voice dripped with sarcasm. "That's why every woman in America wants him—because behind the eye candy he's really just a shallow jerk." She sighed deeply. "Well, I can't say that I blame you for taking him up on his offer. I know I would. How long are you going to be gone?"

Lara glanced at the bedside clock. "It's one-thirty in the afternoon here. Graeme had a television interview and some autographing sessions to attend this morning, but he's booked a private jet to take us to London later tonight. We'll drive to Scotland from there. With the time difference, it will be tomorrow afternoon by the time we reach the inn. We'll stay for two days."

"I hope you know what you're doing, Lara."

"Me, too."

"What do you want me to tell Christopher when I see him?"

"Just tell him that I need a little more time to think things through and that I'll call him as soon as I can."

"He said that he tried calling you last night and again this morning, and that you haven't been answering your cell phone."

Lara paused in the process of folding a pair of jeans. "You spoke with him today?"

Val's voice sounded exasperated. "He called me because he was worried about you and wanted to know if I'd heard from you. I had to do some pretty quick thinking to come up with a plausible excuse, I'll have you know."

"What did you tell him?"

"That you hadn't been sleeping well at the beach house and that you'd probably just turned your phone off in order to get a good night's rest."

Lara gave a moan of frustration. "Oh, I hate this. I hate lying to him. He's such a nice guy, and he doesn't deserve how I'm treating him right now."

"So tell him the truth."

"I can't. He'll hate me."

"He won't hate you, Lara. But he'll be angry with you for not being honest with him from the beginning."

"That's what I'm afraid of."

"Don't worry, I'll console him," Val said, her voice teasing. "He really is cute, in a frumpy professor sort of way. I'll bet I could teach him a thing or two about a thing or two."

"Val…" Lara said in warning.

"I'm kidding. Really. But I am going over to the theater this afternoon to do costume fittings with the kids. Do you want me to tell him that I talked with you? Break the news gently to him?"

Lara finished folding her jeans and laid them carefully in her suitcase. "No, thanks. This is something I have to do myself. He's not expecting me back for a couple of more days, so I'll call him when this whole thing is over and I have a better idea of what I'm going to do."

"Okay."

They talked for a few more minutes about the theater program, and especially about little Alayna, who Val insisted was doing fine.

Lara hung up, frowning. For the first time since she'd made the decision to pursue a divorce from Graeme, she knew she wouldn't continue to date Christopher. Regardless of what happened between her and Graeme, she couldn't become seriously involved with a man she wasn't completely in love with. Christopher could give her everything she needed—security, a stable home, and children—but he couldn't give her the one thing she truly craved.

Happiness.

A knock sounded at her door, and Graeme's voice called softly to her from the other side. Lara opened the door, unaccountably shy to see Graeme, now that they had agreed to spend the next two days together. He'd changed his clothes since breakfast, and wore a pale blue shirt of the softest cotton that turned his eyes to turquoise. He'd showered and she caught the tangy scent of his soap as he braced a hand on the doorjamb and let his gaze sweep over her.

Lara had dressed carefully in a sheer floating top of pale green patterned with flowers and paired with jeans and heeled sandals. She'd pulled her hair back into a loose knot, letting several strands escape to curl around her neck.

"You look lovely," he said, "but I prefer to see your hair down, like this." Reaching out, he flicked her hair free from the elastic band, letting it fall around her face. "Much better," he said in soft approval, taking a tendril between his thumb and forefinger and rubbing it thoughtfully. "I like this, too." His fingers dipped briefly into the low neckline of her top and withdrew the locket.

Lara closed her fingers around the locket, and her

hand brushed against Graeme's. Just that brief contact was enough to send her heart rate skipping. How was she ever going to survive two days in close proximity with this man?

More importantly, how was she ever going to let him go, when the time came?

"I'm ready to go," she said, her voice breathless.

"And the papers?"

Lara indicated her case, although she didn't want to think about those divorce papers and what they meant. "I have them with me."

Graeme arched an eyebrow. "Are you sure about this? There's still time to change your mind. And I should warn you about the paparazzi. I'll try to keep a low profile, but there's always a possibility that they'll learn about our plans. If they do, they'll follow us and snap our pictures wherever we go. The gossip tabloids will print things about us that may or may not be true. They'll pry into your past, pester your family and friends, and probably try to paint you in the worst possible light. Nothing will be private." He paused for emphasis. "Nothing."

Lara took a deep breath. "I don't care."

She realized it was no less than the truth. For years she'd waited for this man, longed for him. She needed to find out if her feelings for him were based on fact or fiction, and if it meant enduring the scrutiny of the media, then so be it. She'd let other people force them apart once before, but she wouldn't let it happen again. This time, if they decided to go their separate ways it would be a choice they made together.

"If reporters ask who you are, I'm going to say you're my wife," Graeme warned.

Lara looked at him, shocked. She'd thought he might be joking, but there was no humor in his expression. She hadn't planned on going public with the news of their marriage, hadn't thought that Graeme would want to, either.

"Are you sure you want to do that?" she asked.

"Absolutely."

"But what about your career? You'd break millions of female hearts, not to mention how the media will react."

Graeme gave her a laconic smile. "In cases like this, it's always best to come clean. I think being honest with the media will actually deflect a lot of the negative publicity the news would otherwise draw. Besides, they'd find out about it sooner or later." He paused. "But what about you? How will your boyfriend react if he hears about your marriage on the local news? Maybe you should call him first."

Lara thought of Christopher. How would he feel when he learned about her past? He'd be hurt that she hadn't confided in him, but would he be heartbroken? Somehow, Lara didn't think so. They'd shared an easy camaraderie over the past year, working with the kids at the theater program. He'd helped her with several young adult screenplays that she'd written, and he'd promised to help her market them to different production companies and studios. But when she thought about their relationship, she realized most of what they shared revolved around their mutual interest in writing scripts.

There was so much about herself that she'd never shared with Christopher. For instance, he had no idea that she spent her evenings writing erotic fan fiction about the *Galaxy's End* characters, and she'd preferred not to tell him; he'd think it was pure, unadulterated trash. She could never tell him what the writing meant to her, that her stories represented some of the happiest moments of her life. He'd realize that she'd used her writing as a way to cling to her memories of Graeme.

Now she looked at Graeme. "I'll call him later. My roommate, Val, knows everything, so if he does see anything on the news, she'll be able to fill him in on the details."

Lara saw the skepticism in his raised eyebrows, but he didn't say anything. What would Graeme think if he knew about her writing? If he knew that her fictional stories revolved around him and the character he played in the television series? She hoped he wouldn't find out, because then he'd know that she'd never stopped thinking about him, that she'd actually obsessed about him in way that couldn't be healthy.

She gave Graeme what she hoped was a bright smile. "So by tonight, everyone could know that you have a secret wife. I hope you know what you're doing."

"I know exactly what I'm doing."

"You do realize that I've never traveled as anybody's wife before?"

A slow smile curved his lips. "Trust me, that's no problem. I can show you anything you need to know."

12

At Graeme's insistence, the hotel staff discreetly moved Lara's belongings from her room to his penthouse suite until they were ready to leave for the airport that evening. Lara had watched in amazement; although she'd been accustomed to her father receiving preferential treatment during his days as a prominent politician, that didn't come close to the obsequious service Graeme commanded. It seemed the only person who didn't want to bend over backward to accommodate him was his publicist, Tony Angelini, who wasn't happy to learn that his biggest client was secretly married.

Lara sat curled on the sofa in Graeme's luxurious suite, flipping through a magazine and pretending she wasn't listening as Tony lectured Graeme. She might have been invisible for all the notice he took of her, but for once she didn't mind. The man completely intimidated her with his fierce energy and his even fiercer expression.

"I'm your publicist, and if anyone deserved to know about your marriage it was me, Graeme." He paced the floor of the living room and raked his hand through his black hair. "How could you keep something like this from me? I could have broken this news to the public in a way that could have helped your career. But to have hidden it from me all this time—" He spluttered as he stopped pacing, and glared at Graeme. "Well, quite frankly, it's insulting."

Graeme leaned negligently against a window, staring down at the Las Vegas strip, seemingly impervious to his publicist's tirade.

"Now you tell me that you're going to be gone for the next several days without even a by-your-leave. What am I going to tell David Letterman? If you're a no-show with him then you can forget about getting an invite back to his show."

"Dave and I are friends," Graeme muttered. "He'll understand."

"Dammit, Graeme, are you even listening to me? Do you know how insulting this whole thing is?"

Graeme turned from the window, his gaze shifting briefly to Lara before turning to his agent. "Yeah," he finally said. "I'm listening. Although quite frankly, I don't see what you find so insulting. My private is life is just that—private. If I choose to keep my marriage under wraps, then it's nobody's business but mine and my wife's."

Tony gave a disbelieving laugh. "Do you have any clue what this could do to your career?" He ignored the warning tone in Graeme's voice. "Your popularity has everything to do with the fact that you were single. As in *not married*. Look at what happened to Ben Affleck and Matt Damon after they took themselves off the market. Why do you think George Clooney hasn't married? Do you think anyone is writing steamy stories about *them* on the Internet? There's a reason why your fan Web sites are so hot right now,

Graeme, and it's not because you've been secretly married for the past five years!"

At the mention of steamy Internet stories, Lara stiffened and her startled gaze flew to Tony. There was no way he could be talking about the stories that she wrote. Could he? Her heart began to pound and her hands felt clammy with dread as she determinedly bent her head to her magazine.

But Tony wasn't paying any attention to her. From the corner of her eye, Lara saw him throw his hands up in utter disgust. "Okay, fine. I can see I'm not going to get through to you on this. I've done what I can to keep your ratings up, but I'm not sure this is something we could recover from."

Graeme stared at Tony as if the other man had sprouted three heads. "Recover from? Tony, this isn't something I need to *recover* from. Frankly, I don't give a damn about the ratings. This is my *life*. And if my being married means I'm no longer appealing to female viewers, then I'm okay with that. Maybe I won't have to attend any more fan festivals! There's only one woman whose opinion I should really care about, if you want to know the truth."

Tony's glance flicked to Lara and away again, but not before she saw the resentment in his eyes, and something else, too. Something that looked like speculation.

"Right. Well, I guess we'll just have to wait until this comes out to see how it'll impact your fan base." He glanced at his watch. "I have to go, kids. Someone has to do damage control with the convention people, and I guess that's what I get paid the big bucks for. Congratulations on your nuptials. Wish me luck when it comes time to explain this to the media."

Lara's eyebrows rose at the condescension in Tony's voice. They watched as the publicist left the suite. Lara tipped her head and considered the closed door. "He's the best publicist in the industry?"

"That's what they say," Graeme agreed.

Lara shivered. "He's a horrible man."

Graeme laughed, but Lara thought it had a hard edge to it. "His methods are a little unorthodox, but he's treated me well. He really wants his clients to succeed, although I'll be the first to admit that sometimes he goes a little too far."

Lara snorted. "Of course he does. If you succeed, he succeeds. Why didn't you put the poor man out of his misery and tell him that you'd be single again very soon?"

"Because I meant what I said. My private life is my own business. Although I wouldn't put it past him to begin digging a little deeper into my past." Graeme gave her a grim smile. "He's probably wondering what else there is that he doesn't know about me."

Lara turned a page of the magazine, pretending to be absorbed by the glossy advertisements. "If being an actor means having your publicist prying into your past, then I'd never survive in Hollywood," she said in a low voice. "I can't imagine having complete strangers knowing the intimate details of my life." She gave a small shudder. "It's creepy."

Graeme lowered his long frame onto the sofa beside Lara. She slid him a sideways glance and saw his eyes narrow as he considered her. "I agree," he said smoothly. "I've never understood why anyone would care what I ate for dinner the night before or who I shared it with. Then there are the fans who can't separate me from the characters I portray. They think I *am* Kip Corrigan, and they expect me to behave like him when I'm in public." He gave a huff of laughter. "They're actually affronted when I don't."

Lara felt a pang of sympathy for Graeme. She'd never really considered how his life must be. Just running an errand could become a game of duck-and-hide from the fans and the paparazzi.

"It must be difficult," she murmured. "Like having a dual identity."

"You should know all about that," he said softly.

Lara snapped her head up to stare at Graeme. "Excuse me?"

"After all," he continued, as if she hadn't spoken, "you're a professional when it comes to hiding yourself—your true self—from people, even those closest to you." He paused meaningfully. "Especially those closest to you."

Lara flushed. "That's not fair, Graeme. I already told you why I lied to you back then. If you can't accept that I was young and foolish and afraid of losing you, then I'm sorry. I don't know what else to say."

Graeme leaned across the cushion that separated them, until she could see the amazing striation of blues and greens in his irises. "I'm not just talking about how you lied to me all those years ago, Lara. I'm talking about who you are today, especially considering your, uh, extracurricular activities during the past few years."

What?

Lara stared at him, completely bemused. "I don't know what you're talking about. Extracurricular activities?" She gave a short laugh. "If you really knew me, then you'd know that I only go out with Christopher on the weekends, and he's never even spent the night at my place. When we do go out, it's usually just for dinner or maybe a movie. So whatever is you *think* I'm doing at night, you're mistaken."

To her dismay, Graeme smiled slowly. "Oh, I'm not mistaken, *Secret Lover.* I know all about the erotic stories you write and post to the Internet. I know that every one of them features Kip Corrigan in the flesh, so to speak. I wonder if you've shared that little detail of your life with your boyfriend?"

Lara felt the color drain from her face, and her stomach did an odd little inversion. He knew about her fan fiction! Her mind worked rapidly, trying to recall a time when she might have slipped up and done something to reveal her true identity online. But no, there was no way. *She'd been so careful.*

"I don't know what you're talking about," she fibbed, but she knew the truth was there in her face, and in the oh so casual tone of her voice.

"Oh, I think you do," Graeme said silkily, and reaching out, he tugged the magazine from her nerveless fingers. "I still remember the story you let me read back in London. It was very good, as I recall, but tame in comparison to what you're writing now. But your voice hasn't changed a bit."

"You read my stories," she breathed.

The implications stunned her.

Graeme flipped the magazine onto the coffee table and stretched one arm along the length of the couch behind her. His eyes gleamed with an unholy light. "Yeah. I did."

Lara stared at him, speechless. "How did you discover them? And what makes you think it was me who wrote them?"

"Tony likes to monitor fan Web sites." He shrugged. "He says it helps him stay on his game. Anyway, he came across your stories and was pretty blown away by how popular they were." He arched an eyebrow at her. "I knew right away that it was you who'd written them. Especially after reading that one story where Kip and Lily spend two nights trapped together in the prison cell."

"Oh." Now it was Lara's turn to flush. She remembered that story clearly as it was one of her personal favorites. She also knew why Graeme had recognized the story; she'd drawn it directly from her experiences with him.

"Yeah, *oh,*" he said, noting her expression. "Jesus, Lara, where did you learn to write stuff like that? I mean, we never even had a chance to do some of the things you describe in those stories."

Was that regret she heard in his voice? Did he actually want to do some of the things the characters in her stories had done? The mere thought caused ribbons of desire to unfurl low in her abdomen, and a slow throb began to build between her thighs.

"I did, um, research," she admitted, and then as his face darkened, "Not that kind! I only meant that I did a lot of reading. I never did any hands-on research, if that's what you're thinking."

"I know."

Lara stopped breathing. "What do you mean, *you know?* How could you know?"

She watched, stunned, as Graeme pinched the bridge of his nose and considered his response. Finally, he let out a hard breath and looked at her. "Let's just say that I've kept tabs on you. You said you hadn't slept with Christopher, and I know you weren't involved with anyone before him. You're right about him, by the way. He's a nice guy and he's treated you well." He smiled. "Almost like you were his own sister."

Lara could only stare at him, too shocked even to speak. Too shocked to take offense at his suggestion that Christopher treated her more like a sister than a lover. His admission rocked her all the way to her toes. She'd been so certain that once she'd returned to the States he'd moved on with his life and hadn't given her so much as a second thought.

"So what…you spied on me? Or hired a private investigator to follow me around and pry into my private life?"

Graeme made a low growling sound of frustration and scrubbed a hand over his hair. "I needed to know that you were okay. You were so young. What if I'd gotten you pregnant? I knew damned well that neither you nor your father would tell me, and I had a right to know."

Lara dragged in a deep breath and found her voice. "Well, I wasn't pregnant."

"I know."

Again, she thought she detected a note of regret in his voice. A rush of pleasure coursed through her. He had wanted to know she was okay. The knowledge that he'd cared enough to try and find her gave her courage.

"So…you read my stories," she repeated, turning on the sofa to face him. She uncurled one leg from beneath her and lowered it to the floor, opening herself to him.

His expression sharpened, and his eyes darkened with heat. "Yeah, I did."

Lara drew in a deep breath, recalling the feeling of sexual power and confidence that she'd had when she and Graeme had been in the elevator the night before. When she had promised to fulfill his every desire. Right now, she needed that confidence.

"So…which of my stories did you read?" she asked, carefully studying his face. She waited, breathless, for his response, but was unprepared when he slid his hand beneath her hair and cupped the nape of her neck. His big hand was warm and rough against her skin and she shivered in anticipation, mesmerized by what she saw in his eyes.

"All of them." He searched her face, before dropping his gaze to her mouth. He stroked the pad of his thumb over her lower lip. "I read them all. If it's Kip Corrigan you want…"

Lara stared at him, unable to move, unable to breathe.

Graeme dragged his gaze upward and for a brief, terrible instant she saw the raw pain in his eyes. It was gone in a flash and Lara wondered if she had imagined it. Then he did the last thing she expected him to do.

He pulled away.

"If it's Kip Corrigan you want, then I'm sorry, love. I'm not him."

Silence stretched between them, and Lara knew she should say something.

Anything.

Assure him that she didn't want Kip. She'd never wanted Kip. She only wanted Graeme.

But before she could collect her wits enough to speak, he rose to his feet in one fluid movement, his expression shuttered.

"I'll go check on our transportation," he muttered, and he left the suite, closing the door quietly but firmly behind him.

THE FOLLOWING DAY, Lara stared out of the passenger window of Graeme's car at the inn where she and Graeme had spent two days and nights secluded in a small room following their elopement. Nothing had changed in the five years since she'd last seen the small Scottish inn, and the stone manor house retained all of the quaint charm she remembered.

Autumn leaves carpeted the lawn with hectic color along either side of the gravel drive, and the hand-painted wooden sign that hung over the entrance looked exactly the same. Glancing up, her eyes sought the casement windows of the room where she and Graeme had stayed, and her chest tightened. Bunches of ivy dangled out of the window boxes beneath the leaded panes, and several mourning doves roosted on the tiled roof directly above.

Their flight had been uneventful and mostly silent, as Graeme had hunkered down in his seat, crossed his arms over his chest and closed his eyes. Lara didn't know if he'd really slept or if he'd only wanted to avoid conversation with her, but she'd felt very much alone.

She'd replayed their conversation over and over again in her head, realizing that he'd tried to tell her how much he disliked being compared to his fictional character, Kip Corrigan. He wanted to be recognized and appreciated for who he was, not who he pretended to be on television, and she'd completely botched it.

By the time they were in the car and on their way to Scotland, the opportunity to talk about the moment had passed and Lara didn't see any way to bring it up again. Graeme had been courteous and friendly, but there was an aloofness to him that had been absent at the Las Vegas hotel, almost as if he deliberately kept a part of himself withdrawn from her.

Lara didn't know how they would ever get through the next two days, considering how estranged she felt from him. There was a part of her that seriously considered handing over the divorce papers for his signature then and there. There seemed no point in rehashing old memories.

"Well, here we are," Graeme commented, peering through the windshield at the inn, before arching one eyebrow at Lara. "The scene of the crime."

Lara pulled her gaze away from the house and turned to look at him, her tone serious. "I never thought I'd be back here."

They'd arrived at Heathrow Airport, where they'd been greeted by airport security personnel and escorted through a private exit to a waiting car. By the time the paparazzi realized he was there, Graeme and Lara were already on the motorway, speeding their way toward Scotland. Lara wasn't sure she'd ever become accustomed to the preferential treatment that Graeme received wherever he went. But he hardly seemed to notice; he was appreciative and thankful for whatever assistance was offered, without seeming pompous or insincere.

"I'll get the luggage," he said, but made no move to open his door. "Hey."

Lara drew in a deep breath and smiled at him. "I'm okay. This just brings back so many memories, you know?"

Reaching over, he covered her hand with his own, gently squeezing her fingers. "I hope they're not all bad memories."

Lara knew he referred to that morning when her father had discovered them together and forcibly separated them. She could still recall how she'd felt as she'd been hustled into a waiting car, wondering what horrible things her father might be saying to Graeme.

She followed Graeme into the lobby of the inn, her eyes roaming over the dark paneling and lingering on the many animals that had been stuffed and mounted for display. Dozens of pairs of eyes stared down at her, everything from ferrets and badgers, to foxes. Lara had forgotten this particular aspect of the inn. So much for her rose-colored glasses. They hadn't gotten past the lobby and already her memories were being debunked.

She shuddered.

If Graeme thought the taxidermy display was strange, he gave no indication. As he spoke with the innkeeper, Lara wandered across the lobby. A sturdy staircase curved toward the upper floors, and across from the registration desk, a double door opened into a small pub. Lara still remembered sharing a meal with Graeme in the cozy darkness of the pub, before she'd gone up to their room to prepare for her wedding night.

Poking her head inside, she saw a slender young man stacking clean glasses behind the bar. He looked up, and Lara guessed he was no older than her. His dark hair was unfashionably long and slicked back, except for an unruly lock that fell over his forehead.

"Hello. Just arriving?" he asked.

Lara looked over at Graeme as he registered them at the front desk. "Yes, we are."

"Ah, you're American." He grinned and braced his hands on the bar. "We'll be opening shortly. Why don't you come down fer a drink after ye're settled in?"

"Thank you, maybe we will." Lara gave him a brief smile and joined Graeme at the front desk.

He glanced at her as he signed the registration paperwork and his eyes narrowed. "You look exhausted. There's time enough for you to catch a quick nap before dinner."

"That sounds like a good idea," she murmured, realizing just how tired she was. She hadn't slept on the flight, and had been too edgy during the long ride to Scotland to do much more than catnap. Now she yawned hugely. "Sorry. I didn't realize how tired I was until you mentioned it."

"We'll be needing a meal," Graeme said to the innkeeper, not taking his eyes from Lara's face.

"We serve a delicious steak and kidney pie in the pub, and we have six local drafts on tap," offered the innkeeper, an attractive middle-aged woman. She gave Graeme a wink. "A braw mon like yersel, wi' such a bonny wife, needs tae keep his strength up."

Lara felt her face heat with color at the woman's knowing look, not daring to look at Graeme.

He hefted Lara's suitcase in one hand and his duffel bag in the other. "Thanks. Do you have a menu for room service? We've been traveling for the better part of twelve hours. I think we'll turn in early."

"There's a menu in the room," the woman smiled. "The kitchen is open until nine o'clock."

Lara climbed the stairs, acutely conscious of Graeme behind her. In just a few minutes they would be back in the room where they'd spent their wedding night. But she couldn't envision the two of them sharing the kind of intimacy they'd shared five years ago, not when he seemed so distant. So remote.

"Here we are."

They'd stopped in front of a heavy, paneled door and Lara waited as Graeme fitted the key into the lock and turned the handle. Then he pushed the door open and stood back for her to enter.

Lara drew in a deep breath, and as she stepped through the door, memories of the two unforgettable nights of five years earlier washed over her.

13

LATE-AFTERNOON sunlight filtered in through the casement windows, dappling the bed and floor in wavy patterns of light. Lara stood in the center of the room and let the memories of their wedding night wash over her.

Nothing had changed. An antique iron sleigh bed, heaped with tartan-covered pillows and looking oh so tempting with its lofty down comforter, dominated the room.

An image pushed itself into her head, and for an instant, she was helpless to resist it. Graeme, his face darkly flushed, the muscles in his arms standing out in strong relief as he braced himself over her. Graeme, thrusting into her, his skin like hot silk as he slid against her. Kissing her neck, and then laving her nipple—

"I'll run a bath for you."

Lara snapped back to reality at Graeme's words. She turned to see he had set their luggage down beside the bed. Without looking at her, he crossed the room to an adjoining door and a moment later she heard the water running. In the uncanny way he had, Graeme seemed to know what she needed before she realized it herself. A bath sounded like sheer heaven.

She glanced around the rest of the room. More tartan

covered the two parlor chairs tucked into the corner, and the walls were a collage of framed oil paintings depicting fruit bowls and pastoral scenes.

"It's exactly as I remember it," Lara said, dropping her laptop case and pocketbook onto one of the decorative chairs. "I don't think anything has changed, not even the blankets."

"Let's hope they've laundered them since we were last here," Graeme said drily, coming back into the bedroom. He surveyed the room with a critical eye. If he felt any of the same emotions that Lara did upon seeing the room again, he gave no indication.

"So, here we are," Lara said, striving for a normal tone. "Do you remember how I wouldn't let you come upstairs until after I'd had a bath?"

"I remember very much wanting to help you with that bath." Graeme smiled. "I told you that I'd have one beer in the pub, and then I was coming up whether you were finished or not."

"I wasn't quite finished."

"I don't think I let you finish."

For a brief moment neither of them spoke, recalling what had happened after that. Heat warmed Graeme's eyes, and Lara felt a responding simmer low in her pelvis.

She dragged her gaze away and forced herself to focus on the present. "I'll check the bath water," she mumbled.

But as she turned toward the bathroom, she was acutely aware of Graeme's eyes on her. What was he thinking of the two nights they'd once spent in this very room? Did he remember how magical and amazing they had been? Until her wedding night, Lara had never slept in the same bed with a man, and she could still recall the wonder of having Graeme there beside her, touching her. Even when her body had been sated, she'd been unable to sleep, too aware of him to fully relax. Instead, she'd lain awake and watched him, until he stirred and pulled her into his arms and loved her with a fierce tenderness that had stolen her breath.

The bathroom hadn't changed in five years, and Lara had to smother a laugh when she saw the same small tub that she and Graeme had once shared. He'd been determined to do everything together that weekend, even bathe. He was bigger now than he'd been five years ago, and Lara noted with regret that there wouldn't be enough room in the tub for him alone, never mind the two of them.

Leaning over the tub, she tried to turn the knob off but it was stuck. Already, water threatened to slosh over the sides of the tub and onto the tiled floor. She grunted with effort and in the next instant, Graeme set her aside and bent over to easily close the faucets. The movement caused his jeans to pull snug across his backside, and Lara stood back to admire his taut butt.

"One thing hasn't changed," he said, straightening. "The plumbing is still faulty." His eyes drifted over her. "You're soaking wet."

Following his gaze, Lara looked down at herself to see that her entire front was wet from where she'd leaned across the full tub. The sheer fabric of the blouse clung to her skin, revealing more than it concealed.

Lara made a sound of distress and plucked the material away from her body, uncomfortably aware of how damp the fabric was now that the water had cooled.

"Here, let's do this." Before Lara could guess his intent, Graeme grasped the hem of her blouse and drew it over her head until she stood in front of him in just her bra and jeans. Her first instinct was to cover herself, but then she saw the heated expression in Graeme's eyes.

Slowly, she lowered her arms.

GRAEME LET the blouse drop to the floor, unable to take his eyes from Lara.

So beautiful.

She didn't move when he slid his hands up the length of her arms and over her shoulders, feeling the fragile line of her collarbones beneath his fingers. Finally, he cradled her face in his hands, letting his gaze linger on each feature, memorizing her. Her breathing had quickened, and beneath his hand, he could feel the tiny, frantic beating of her pulse.

"Lara," he murmured, liking the feel of her name on his lips.

Her breathing hitched at the sound of her name, and as he watched, her eyelashes fluttered and her mouth parted. He'd fantasized about this so many times, about being with her, here in this very inn. But in his dreams, she was his for more than just two days.

She was his forever.

He'd wanted this for so long, but he needed Lara to want *him.* Not Kip Corrigan. Not some fantasy lover. Not any of the characters he'd portrayed during his career. He wanted this to be about him and Lara.

"I came here for you," he said, his voice roughened by emotion. "For this. I came here because I haven't been able to stop thinking about that summer, and I needed to know if it really was as good as I remembered."

She made a murmur of assent and moved closer to him. Her fingers came to rest on his rib cage and he could feel the heat of her hands through the thin fabric of his shirt. He knew she was exhausted, had just spent the last half day traveling with little to no sleep, but he found he wasn't strong enough to let her take her bath and go to bed as he'd planned.

He wanted her with a fierce urgency that he couldn't ignore. He wanted to relive that long-ago weekend, to relearn all the curves and secret places of her body, to recall the sounds she'd made as he loved her and the expression on her face as he brought her pleasure.

"Graeme," she whispered, and her hands crept upward to cup his neck and urge his head down.

Her lips were incredibly soft, her kisses full and moist as her tongue pushed hotly against his own and sent a current of desire straight to his groin.

She pressed more fully against him, and Graeme could feel the sweet fullness of her breasts against his chest. His hands slid down the length of her back, exploring and discovering the curve and bumps of her spine, and the indent at the small of her back, just above the waistband of her jeans. Everything about her was so familiar and yet so new.

He slanted his mouth across hers, opening her to delve more deeply, to drink her in. She moaned and shifted in his arms, and behind the zipper of his jeans, his erection swelled.

Without breaking the kiss, her fingers worked the buttons of his shirt slowly and surely, until she tugged the shirttails free from his jeans and pushed the garment from his shoulders.

"Mmm," she moaned against his mouth, her hands smoothing over his chest. "You feel so good."

Graeme broke the kiss and leaned back to look at her. The silver locket nestled in the valley between her breasts, and the lacy bra only heightened his rising desire, cradling her breasts the way his hands longed to do.

"I was going to wait," he admitted. "To let you make the first move. I didn't want this to be about sex, but I can't seem to control myself when you're around."

Lara gave him a wobbly smile. "I don't want you to control yourself, not now."

The bathroom was too small for Graeme to do what he would have liked, which was to sweep her up in his arms and carry into the bedroom. So instead he lifted her up, letting her hook her legs around his hips as he cradled her bottom. She wrapped her arms around his neck and hung on. With their lips fused together, he walked with her into the next room and backed her up to the mattress, laying her across the plaid comforter and following her with the length of his body.

His hands trembled as he flicked the closure of her bra open and drew the garment from her body. Her nipples tightened beneath his fingers, and then he worked his way lower, to the fastening of her jeans. Lara tunneled her fingers through his hair, urging him on as he pressed hot, desperate kisses against her breasts, her stomach, her hip bones.

"Please, please," she panted. She made tiny mewling sounds of pleasure as he slid a hand between her legs and cupped her through the denim. She squirmed against his hand, and he rubbed her clitoris as he tormented first one nipple, and then the next with his mouth and tongue.

He unsnapped her jeans and then the zipper rasped down. Lara lifted her hips, helping him to push the pants down over her legs, kicking them free along with her panties and sandals, and then she was gloriously naked beneath him.

Graeme wanted to worship her with his body, to demonstrate to her that she was his until she no longer had any doubt about where she belonged.

He slid his hand between her legs, sliding his finger along her hot, slick cleft as he kissed her hungrily. She gave a low, keening cry and arched her hips against his hand, seeking more contact, and Graeme knew it wouldn't take much to bring her to climax.

"No, not like this," he said, breaking their kiss. "I want to be inside you, love."

"Yes, I want that, too," she panted, and her fingers went with unerring skill to his waistband.

Graeme stood up and swiftly yanked off his shoes and socks, and then Lara sat up and helped him push his pants down with hands that visibly trembled. That small sign of her passion nearly undid Graeme.

He'd spent so many years feeling angry.

Lonely.

Empty.

But seeing the physical proof of Lara's need for him was enough for him to forgive her for the hurts of the past.

None of it had been her fault.

She'd wanted him enough to lie about her age and risk her family's anger by eloping with him. If anyone was to blame, he was. He should have stood by her side. He should have refused to let her go. He should have told her father how much he loved her, and that he'd never do anything to prevent her from achieving her dreams.

Instead, he'd let his damnable pride get in the way, and he'd nearly lost the only good thing in his life.

Lara.

Sweet, lovely Lara.

She knelt on the bed and her hand went to his aching shaft, encircling him and stroking him until he thought he might lose it right there.

"Lara, love," he said, on a choked laugh, "I'm not going to last if you do that."

With a secret smile, Lara pulled away and lay back on the mattress, watching him through heavy eyelids. "Then come here," she invited, and patted the bed. She let one leg fall open and Graeme gritted his teeth against the erotic sight of her.

So lovely.

Graeme reached for his discarded jeans and fished in the back pocket for his wallet, pulling a condom free. Tearing it open with his teeth, he covered himself expertly. Then he lowered himself to her side and pulled her close, relishing the feel of her supple body against his. She rolled against him, sliding one leg over his hip and bringing him to the entrance of her body.

"Lara," he muttered, "I'm sorry, love, but I can't wait."

Rolling her beneath him, he dipped his hand between her legs, feeling her slick heat. He inserted a finger into her tightness, watching her face twist with pleasure.

He was breathing hard, trying with difficulty to control his raging passion, but seeing Lara's body flush with her impending orgasm was almost more than he could bear.

"I'm so close," Lara moaned. "Please, please...I need you inside me."

Graeme raised himself over her and positioned himself at her opening. She stared up at him through hazy eyes, and her hands went to his hips, urging him on.

Graeme eased himself inside, wanting to prolong the moment, to draw out her pleasure and watch her come undone. Her head rolled on the pillow and cords stood out on her neck as she strove for deeper contact, but Graeme held her hips still with his hands. With excruciating slowness, he filled her. His back ached with the control it took not to come immediately. Her body was a hot, tight fist around him, and the sensation was so intense that Graeme thought he might die from the pleasure-pain of holding back.

"Ah, Graeme!" she cried, and he relented, plunging into her wetness, and then withdrawing to plunge again.

Lara drew her legs back and he hooked them over his elbows, opening her body so that he could thrust deeper. Harder. She opened her eyes and looked at him, and he used his free hand to cup her jaw and run his thumb over her lower lip.

She caught his finger in her mouth and sucked on it, drawing on it as if it was his cock, swirling her tongue over the pad until he groaned and felt his balls draw up tight in exquisite pleasure.

She held his fingers against her mouth with one hand while the other clutched at his hip, pressing him deeper. He felt her inner muscles tighten around him, contracting and sucking him in, and he couldn't hold back any longer. With a hoarse cry, he exploded in a surge of pleasure that seemed to go on and on, jerking him in helpless waves until finally, he collapsed against Lara, their harsh breathing the only sound in the tiny room.

They lay together for a long, quiet time, while Lara lazily stroked his back and he inhaled her fragrance and the musky scent of their lovemaking.

The last bit of daylight had faded from the room, casting them in deepening shadows, when Graeme finally roused himself enough to discard the condom and drag the covers over them. Then, with Lara tucked neatly against his body, they slept. His last thought before he let sleep take him was that this felt right. He was finally with the woman he wanted to be with.

"DO YOU KNOW how many times I've thought of this room? Of that night?" Graeme's warm voice slid into her ear and curled its way through her body, all the way to her toes.

With a contented sigh, Lara leaned back against Graeme's chest and lazily rubbed a soapy washcloth over the exposed island of his knee. Despite her protests, Graeme had proven that they could both fit into the cramped bathtub.

They had slept through the night and then ordered breakfast in their room, the way they had done five years earlier. Then they'd returned to bed, reenergized. Reinvigorated. Lara still blushed when she thought of what she and Graeme had done. In broad daylight, no less, with the poor housekeeper running the vacuum cleaner directly outside the door of their room. Lara hadn't been quiet and, in the end, neither had Graeme.

Now it was early evening, and they'd finally roused themselves enough to take a bath before going downstairs to the pub for dinner.

"Mmm," she said, admiring the layers of thigh muscle beneath the whorls of wet hair. "But I'm betting you didn't think about this incredibly tiny bathtub."

She shifted her position, only to have Graeme give a pained groan. "Careful, love, if you want me to give you bairns."

Lara stilled for a moment, and then resumed swirling the washcloth over his leg, keeping her tone carefully neutral. "Do you want children, Graeme?"

"Do you?"

"I think I asked you first."

"You do realize, love, that we had unprotected sex in Las Vegas. There's a possibility I've already impregnated you."

Lara swallowed hard at the thought of carrying Graeme's child, and her heart constricted painfully. Given where she was in her cycle, she knew the likelihood of becoming pregnant was slim to none. She twisted her head around to look at him. "I would never try to trap you into marriage, Graeme."

He looked at her in amusement, and Lara realized what she'd said. "Oh, right," she murmured, chagrined. "I already did that."

Graeme tightened his arms around her, one big hand cupping a breast and toying with the nipple. "It's okay, love. I've had five years to grow accustomed to the idea and I find I'm rather liking it."

Lara turned on her side to see him better, heedless

of the water that sloshed over the edges of the tub. "What are you saying?"

Graeme shrugged. "That it's better than I remembered."

Lara didn't need to ask him what he meant. Everything about their return visit to Scotland had been better than she remembered. Since making love to her the night before, Graeme hadn't let her out of his arms. She was deliciously sore from his potent lovemaking, but she wasn't about to complain. She wanted to savor every second of their time together, and to hear him admit that these two days had exceeded his expectations filled her with a fierce joy. "I'm in total agreement with you," she said, and pressed a kiss against his wet collarbone.

Graeme gripped her arms to help her maintain her balance, but when Lara put her hand down to shift position, her hand brushed against the unmistakable rise of his erection. Her eyes widened.

"How do you do that?"

He smiled, all innocence. "Trust me, love, it's easy with you."

He lifted her up until she straddled him, and Lara's breath caught at the sensation of their slippery bodies sliding against each other.

"Oh," she said softly. Dipping her hand into the warm water, she gripped him, reveling in how he jerked against her palm.

He leaned his head back against the edge of the tub, and Lara couldn't help but admire the strong column of his throat and the powerful thrust of his shoulders, gleaming wetly from the bath water. He watched her through slitted eyes, and Lara could almost feel the heat simmering in their translucent depths.

When one strong hand snaked through the water and began teasing her, she gasped once in surprise, and then again in pleasure. Graeme parted her sleek folds, his finger skating over the nub of her clitoris and awakening her desire. He rubbed it carefully, deliberately, until Lara rose up on her knees and leaned forward, draping herself over Graeme's torso.

She shuddered softly as his lips teased her earlobe, biting gently and then soothing the sensitized skin with his tongue.

"Graeme," she protested weakly, "you're killing me."

"Mmm," he hummed in agreement.

"All I can think about is touching you...tasting you." Beneath the water, she still gripped him strongly, smoothing her thumb over the blunted head of his penis, while he buried his face in her neck and pressed his lips along the sensitive length of her neck. "I can't get enough of you."

She felt him smile against her skin, and then he inserted a finger inside her. Lara shivered.

"You're so slippery and your skin's so hot," he rasped. He crooked his finger gently and Lara cried out at the explosion of sensation. "Ah, there's your G-spot," he murmured in satisfaction. "Before we're through, I intend to find them all."

Lara raised herself up and he withdrew his hand, cupping and squeezing her bottom instead, and exploring the crease of her buttocks. Lara gasped when he skimmed a single finger across her bottom, and her sex swelled in response, pulsing strongly with need. She moaned softly and positioned his shaft at her opening, sliding herself back and forth over his engorged length.

"Oh, yeah," he breathed, his voice warm in her ear. "You make me crazy for you. But this isn't going to work, love. We need protection." Supporting her with one hand, he reached over the edge of the tub, stretching toward the two condoms that Lara had placed on the edge of the sink. With a desperate lunge that nearly brought him out of the tub and Lara along with him, he snagged one of the little packets in his fingers.

"Success," he grinned, as Lara rebalanced herself against him.

Lara watched doubtfully as he tore open the foil packaging. "Do those work underwater?"

"I have to think it's better than using nothing," Graeme said. "Here, slide back a bit."

Lara scooted back on his thighs and watched as he raised his hips until he broke the surface of the water. The sight of him turned her bones weak, and with unsteady fingers, she helped him cover himself.

Turning his face, he captured her lips in a kiss that was searingly hot. Lara groaned and in one smooth movement, slid down over his hard flesh, reveling in how he stretched her, filled her.

This was what she had been longing for—this man in her arms, driving her wild with the things he did to her. She curled her hands around his neck and pressed moist, fevered kisses along his jaw, all the while pumping her hips over him, water sloshing, feeling herself draw tighter and closer to release. His lips slanted across hers and she welcomed the intrusion of his tongue, wanting to be closer still.

His big hands cupped her bottom, spreading her cheeks and tormenting her a bit before squeezing them gently. He dragged his mouth from hers, his breathing fast and uneven. "Have I told you how much I love your arse?"

"Not lately," she said between hard pants, and chewed her lower lip, concentrating on the pressure that was building between her legs and swirling to a point of excruciating pleasure.

"How's this?" Graeme asked, and then his hand was on her mons, pressing down on where they were joined, increasing the pressure and making her aware of every hard, hot slide of his flesh inside her. When he stroked his thumb over the swollen rise of her clitoris, she gave a strangled cry and her orgasm crashed over her in waves, so that she was only dimly aware of Graeme, thrusting strongly upward and shouting as he was swept along with her.

Her last coherent thought was that she needed this man in the same way she needed air to breathe, and she wanted so much more than just a weekend.

She wanted a lifetime of weekends.

14

"ARE YOU SURE you don't want to have a meal delivered to the room? Someone is bound to recognize you if we eat dinner in the pub." Lara stood in front of a mirror and coiled her hair into a loose bun, feeling refreshed and relaxed after a nap. Not to mention the amazing sex. If she weren't so hungry, Lara thought she could willingly spend their entire visit to Scotland in their hotel room.

Graeme lounged on the bed, flipping through a magazine as he waited for Lara to finish getting ready. "Maybe not. I've found I'm not nearly as interesting here as I am in the States."

Lara looked at him in the mirror's reflection. "You're kidding, right? You're a gorgeous guy. Any woman with a pulse will find you interesting. Don't forget, I've seen your fan Web sites. Trust me," she said drily, "you'll be recognized."

Graeme swung his legs to the floor and stood up, crossing the room to stand directly behind her. He looked mouthwateringly handsome in a pair of jeans paired with a black shirt. "Nobody will recognize me here. Besides, we need to make an appearance so that the management doesn't think I'm in here killing you. You scream something fierce when you're aroused."

Lara turned to face him, sliding her hands around his waist, not even remotely embarrassed by his teasing. "Okay, then. I'll do my best to protect you from the hordes of women who'll descend on us once word gets out that you're here."

"I feel so much better," he laughed, pulling her in for a lingering kiss.

As they descended the staircase to the lobby, Lara was acutely conscious of the many stuffed animals with their tiny glass eyes watching her from their perches along the wall.

"Talk about creepy," she whispered to Graeme. "Why don't I remember these from five years ago?"

Graeme eyed a weasel with distaste. "I don't think we made it out of our room long enough to notice the decor in the rest of the inn."

"I hope they don't extend into the pub. I'm not sure I could eat with so many eyes watching me."

Thankfully, the decor in the pub ran to Scottish sports memorabilia and wide-screen televisions over the bar. Graeme and Lara chose a cozy booth in a corner and the bartender that Lara had spoken with earlier came around to their table.

"Evenin', folks. Can I interest you in a local draft?" He smiled at Lara, but when he turned his attention to Graeme, his eyes widened and Lara could have sworn all the color drained from his face.

"I'll have the amber ale," she said, giving Graeme an I-told-you-so look.

When the bartender gave no indication that he'd even heard Lara, Graeme arched an eyebrow at the other man. "Is everything okay?"

The young man visibly pulled himself together. "Oh,

aye. Terribly sorry about that. It's just that you look so much like this bloke on television." Jerking his gaze from Graeme, he fixed his attention on the small notepad he held in his hand. "An amber ale," he repeated, his gaze flicking between the two of them. "And for you, sir?"

Graeme gave Lara an amused look. "I'll have the same."

"Verra well. I'll bring those right over."

He turned abruptly away and Lara covered her mouth to hide her smile. "Nobody will recognize you, huh?"

Graeme stared after the bartender with a puzzled expression on his face. "He didn't scem especially starstruck. Maybe he's not a *Galaxy's End* fan," hc mused.

"Or maybe his girlfriend *is,* and the poor guy has had to endure listening to her gush about you every Thursday night," Lara teased. "I'd probably hate you, too."

Graeme reached across the table and took her hands. "But you don't."

"Well, only when you do that thing that makes me wild, and then you hold back—"

"Here ye are," interrupted a feminine voice, and they both looked up to see the woman from the reception desk holding their mugs of beer. "Two amber ales." She set the drinks down on the table and beamed at both of them. "Are you settlin' in, then? Is the room to your liking?"

"The room is perfect," smiled Lara. "It's exactly as I remember it."

"Oh, ye've been here before, have ye?"

Lara caught the warning look in Graeme's eyes. "Um, yes, but it was a long time ago."

"The posting inn has been in my family for generations." The woman extended her hand to Lara. "I'm Margaret Dunbar." She gestured toward the bar area. "That's my son, Robbie. I have two daughters who do the cooking. If ye like fish, try the Arbroath smokie or the wild salmon."

"Do you run the inn, then?" Graeme asked, taking a swallow of his beer.

"Aye, these past ten years, since the death of my father. When were ye last here?"

"Five years ago, in August. As I recall, the innkeeper was a bald-headed man with a red beard."

"Ah," she smiled. "That would be my brother. He comes in and works when I'm on vacation." She tapped a finger against her chin. "Five years ago in August, you said? That must have been the weekend that I took young Robbie to university. The one weekend I wasn't here and all hell broke loose. Maybe ye recall that?"

Graeme took a sip of his ale. "No, sorry. What happened?"

The woman waved a dismissive hand. "An elopement, an angry father, the usual." She leaned a hip against their table, relishing her story. "We're verra close to the border here, so we sometimes get young couples from England looking to jump over the anvil. It's not usually anything to talk about, but I guess this father got rather nasty with the bridegroom, threatening all kinds of horrible things."

Lara looked sharply at Graeme, but he was staring at his mug. A frown knitted his brow.

"The lassie was dragged away and the poor lad was near out of his mind, I heard. He made a public spectacle of himself, promising to go after the girl. Ah, young love. Weel, enjoy yer meal," she said, and moved away from their table.

"She might not have been talking about us," Lara whispered, leaning across the table.

Graeme gave her a patient look. "Of course she was talking about us. I made a public scene here in the lobby, challenging your father and promising I'd find you and get you back. It's a wonder they haven't written a bloody ballad about it." He drained his beer.

Lara stared at him. "You told my father you'd come after me?"

Graeme shrugged. "I was young and foolish."

But Lara's heart was pounding so hard it was a wonder he didn't hear it from across the table. "Did you, Graeme? Did you come after me?"

When he looked at her, she saw the bitter regret in his eyes. "Would it have made any difference if I had?"

Lara made a choked sound of dismay. "You know it would have. You don't know what my life was like before I met you.... You were the first person who really saw me. Until you, I'd been invisible. Do you know how hard it was for me to leave you that day? Do you?"

"I told myself it didn't matter." He absently played with the beer coaster. "My life had been going fine before you walked into it." He gave her a rueful smile. "At least, I thought so. But then you came along, like this pure sunbeam in a dusty room, and suddenly I wanted more." Pushing the coaster aside, he leaned forward and Lara was stunned by the intensity of his expression. "I wanted to be the man you believed I was. I wanted to do great things for you. I wanted to capture the moon for you, but that was before I realized that you already had enough money to buy the sun *and* the moon."

Lara made a sound of distress and Graeme covered her hand with his own. "No, let me finish. I told myself that you'd only been slumming when you spent that summer with me. But Christ, you gave me…yourself. And after you left, I couldn't ever look at my life the same way again. Was I angry?" His fingers tightened around hers. "You bet. I wanted to go after you and drag you back by your hair, lock you in a tower like the fairy-tale princess you imagined yourself to be and never let you go."

"Why didn't you?" Lara knew her heart was in her eyes, but she no longer cared.

"I did, Lara. I did."

Lara stared at him in disbelief. "But…how? I never saw you."

He gave a bitter laugh. "My entrance visa was denied. They turned me away in New York and put me on the next flight back to England."

Lara sat back in her seat, speechless. He had come after her. She didn't need to ask why his visa had been denied; she knew enough about the State Department and her father's influence to understand exactly what had happened. She could only imagine how angry Graeme must have been.

"I'm so sorry," she whispered. "I never knew."

Graeme gave her a lopsided grin. "I know, and I don't blame you for any of it."

"Why didn't you write to me? Tell me what had happened?"

"Because I knew the one thing you'd never had was the freedom to make your own choices. I decided that if you wanted to return to me, then it had to be your decision, not mine."

"I can't believe the lengths my father went to in order to keep us apart," she breathed.

"He did it because he loved you, and he didn't think I was good enough for you. Ah, don't cry. I'm here now." Reaching across the table, he swiped away the moisture on her cheek.

"So much of what happened that summer was my own fault," she said miserably. "I should never have lied to you about my age."

Graeme gave a rueful laugh. "I was shocked. You looked so sweet and innocent that I couldn't believe you'd duped me so completely. But in Scotland, a girl can marry when she's sixteen. It doesn't happen very often, mind you, but it does happen. Our marriage was legal in the eyes of the law, and your father knew it. I knew it. Besides, we'd already spent two days together and you weren't a child anymore. If he'd arrived before we'd consummated the marriage then I would most likely have signed his stupid papers, but not after two days of having you in my arms. God forgive me, Lara, but I couldn't let you go."

Lara drew in a deep breath, her eyes locked with his. "How did you finally get your visa approved?"

Graeme smiled grimly. "Money talks. After the pilot episode of *Galaxy's End* aired, it became a whole lot easier to find a lawyer who was willing to investigate the issue and have my visa approved. But by then, three years had passed and I'd given up on ever getting you back. I told myself that I'd moved on with my life."

Lara looked down at their linked hands. "That's what I told myself, too."

"Excuse me, but yer meals are here."

Startled, they broke apart to see Margaret standing by their table, a steaming plate in each hand. She placed their food on the table, but didn't leave. She clasped her hands in front of her and turned hopeful eyes on Graeme.

"I don't know why I didn't see it immediately, but might I say what an honor and a privilege it is to have ye staying at our inn, Mr. Hamilton?"

Lara glanced at Graeme. He looked both amused and resigned. "Thank you very much. I'm glad to be here."

"My son recognized ye first. We're both huge fans of yer work, and I was wondering if ye might be willing to sign an autograph or two?"

"Of course."

Lara watched as the woman gestured frantically at her son, who came around from the end of the bar with two pictures in his hands. He laid them down on the table and Lara saw they were publicity photos of Graeme as Kip Corrigan.

"I knew it was you as soon as I came to take yer order," the young man acknowledged, "so I printed these from the Internet in the hopes that ye might sign them."

Graeme shot Lara a wry look. "You were right."

Lara smiled and folded her hands in her lap and watched as he signed the pictures in bold, scrawling print. He handed them back to the young man who grinned his thanks.

"So this is what your life is like," mused Lara. "You handle it very well."

Graeme gave her a rueful smile as he took a bite of

his salmon. "I'm on my best behavior. I'm not always so accommodating, I'm afraid."

Lara tipped her head and looked at him. "Why are you on your best behavior?"

Before he could answer, Margaret approached their table again, and Lara could almost see Graeme brace himself for another request.

"I'm sorry to disturb ye," she said, "but there's a lady in the lobby asking for ye."

"For me?" Graeme looked genuinely surprised.

"Well, actually, she's looking for yer *wife*."

"For me?" Lara echoed in astonishment. Nobody knew she was in Scotland except— "Valerie!"

The other woman stood in the doorway of the pub, peering at the tables until she spotted Lara. Her face cleared and she quickly made her way toward their table.

"Oh, Lara, I'm so glad I found you!" She stopped at their table, breathless and looking uncharacteristically rumpled.

Lara shot to her feet, taking in Val's bright eyes and disheveled appearance. "Valerie, what is it? Are you okay?"

"Christopher is parking the car. He'll be here any minute!"

Lara felt her heart turn over in her chest. "Christopher is here? In Scotland?"

"I know, right?" Valerie flapped her hand. "I couldn't dissuade him from coming, but he's right behind me and I wanted to at least give you a little bit of warning." Her glance flicked to Graeme, who had stood up, and Lara saw her friend's eyes go a little hazy at the sight of him.

"Why didn't you call me?" Lara demanded, catching Val's elbow and drawing the other woman down into the booth.

"Why didn't you turn your cell phone on?" Val hissed back, smiling sweetly at Graeme.

Lara silently acknowledged that her friend had a point. "Val, this is Graeme Hamilton."

Valerie gave a nervous twitter of laughter and stretched her hand across the table toward Graeme. "It's such a pleasure to finally meet you! I've heard all about you of course, and—"

Lara gave her a hard elbow, and Val abruptly closed her mouth. "Valerie is my roommate," she explained, seeing Graeme's bemusement.

"Ah."

"How did you know where to find us?"

Valerie gave Lara a tolerant look. "I've only had to listen to you talk about this place about a gazillion times." She turned to Graeme. "You may have only spent two days here, but trust me when I say your little getaway made *quite* the impression."

"Valerie!" hissed Lara, mortified. She risked a glance at Graeme, but he was watching Valerie with amusement. When his glance flicked to her, she saw the heat in their depths, and flushed.

"Oh, and here comes Christopher now." Valerie stood up and waved frantically to the man who stood in the entrance of the pub, pushing his glasses up on his nose as he surveyed the room.

Lara watched her former boyfriend cross the pub toward them. He looked even more rumpled and travel weary than Valerie did. He ran a hand distractedly through his hair as he approached their table, and Lara didn't miss how his gaze swept first over her, and then lingered on Graeme, sizing the other man up with an assessing look. He stood at the end of the table, clearly uncomfortable, and cleared his throat. "Hello, Lara."

"Christopher, I—I wasn't expecting to see you here. I don't know what to say." Lara had never felt so awkward before, and she could only guess what he must think of her, knowing she had lied to him about where she was these past several days.

To her surprise, he gave her a gentle smile. "It's okay, Lara. Val explained everything and considering the, uh, unusual circumstances, I completely understand."

"Why are you here?" Lara asked, her gaze sliding between Christopher and Valerie.

To her dismay, Christopher reached inside his jacket pocket and pulled out a newspaper. "This is just a sample of what's on the front page of every gossip rag in the country. The television networks picked it up today."

He tossed the paper onto the table.

There, in enormous headlines, were the words, Graeme Hamilton Makes Secret Deal for Stud Service.

What?

A low growl came from Graeme and he dragged the paper across the table, his expression growing darker with each passing second as he scanned the article.

"What does it say?" Lara asked, dread settling into her bones.

"Lara, honey, we came as soon as we could," Val said. "We didn't want you to see this on the news without any prior warning."

"Well, our marriage is no longer a secret. They know

all about you, and it says here that ye'll grant me a divorce if I agree to give ye a baby in return," snarled Graeme, his Scottish accent becoming more pronounced with his growing displeasure. "The article goes on to say that I'll be single again just as soon as I provide my estranged wife with stud service."

Lara blanched. "But that's impossible. We never—"

"This is Tony's doing," Graeme said grimly, raising his eyes to Lara's.

"But why would he promote such blatant lies? Why would he do this to us?"

"This is his idea of damage control. He wants my fans to think I'll be back on the market again soon, and probably believes this story will boost my ratings." Graeme's voice was dark with displeasure.

Lara's mouth dropped, and she stared at Graeme in disbelief. "How is this damage control? This is the most damaging publicity I've ever seen! Not to mention that it's a complete lie."

Graeme's hand fisted around the newspaper. "Tony has a reputation for enjoying the dramatic. The more media hype surrounding his clients, the better he likes it. He probably thinks he's doing me a favor by assuring my fans that I'll soon be single again, just as soon as I provide ye with stud service, of course."

"Where would he have come up with this idea?" Lara moaned and covered her face with her hands. "It was the waitress at the restaurant that morning, I know it. She must have overheard part of our conversation and talked to someone else, and somehow Tony found out about it."

"Yeah, it wouldn't take long for a rumor like that to circulate through the hotel staff and reach him."

Graeme yanked his cell phone out of his pocket and punched in Tony's number. A moment later, he snapped it shut in frustration. "He's not answering his calls. *Shit*."

"Listen, the paparazzi are probably already on the hunt for you," Christopher said, bracing his hands on the edge of the table. "My suggestion is that Lara come back to the States with us now, before the insanity begins. She can get some clothes together and come stay with me for a while, until this whole thing dies down."

"No." Lara and Graeme both said the word at the same time.

Graeme half rose to from his seat and leaned toward the other man. "I appreciate that you're a *friend* of Lara's, but I'll take care of her," he said tightly. "She won't be staying with you."

Christopher raised both hands in surrender. "Fine. No problem. It was just a suggestion."

At that moment, the innkeeper, Margaret, approached their table. "Will yer friends be joining ye for dinner, then?" she asked, her glance sliding between the four of them.

"Oh, thank you, no," Valerie replied. "We're actually a little jet-lagged." She looked up at Christopher. "Maybe we should just book two rooms and get some sleep, and let Lara and Graeme work this whole thing out."

"Oh, I'm sorry," Margaret interjected, "but we don't have any more rooms available at the moment. This is a popular weekend for travelers and we're fully booked."

Valerie groaned and dropped her head onto her arms.

"Great. This is what I get for trying to be a good friend—stuck in the wilds of Scotland with no place to sleep. Where's William Wallace when you need him?"

"Er, guys? I think you might want to take a look at the television," said Christopher, nodding toward the wide-screen over the bar.

As they watched, a picture of Graeme appeared on the screen and the news anchor launched into a similar version of the story they had just read in the news-paper.

"Christ," muttered Graeme. "I'm going to fire my publicist. Either that, or kill him."

"I should probably tell ye that my son, Robbie, has already told several of his pals that ye're staying here at the inn," Margaret said. "There's no telling who else they've told, but I'd say there's a fair chance we'll have reporters swarming the premises before dark."

A muscle worked in Graeme's cheek as he consid-ered Margaret's words. "All right then," he finally said. "Lara and I will leave now. We can reach London before midnight and be on a private jet back to Chicago from there."

Lara stared at him, appalled, but before she could protest, Margaret spoke.

"I have a better idea," she said, smiling. "My brother runs an inn about twenty kilometers from here where ye can stay. I promise ye this—he won't breathe a word to anyone that ye're there. And yer friends can have yer room here, and get a good night's sleep."

"Oh, no—" Christopher began in an adamant voice, but Valerie abruptly cut him off.

"We'll do it," she said, silencing Christopher with a single, fierce look. She turned to Graeme and Lara.

"This is perfect. Christopher and I will switch places with you. If the paparazzi do show up, they can just hang around waiting for us to make an appearance." She smiled serenely. "Which might not be for several days. Which will provide you with plenty of time to make an escape."

"Excellent," Margaret said. "I'll just send one of the girls up to change the bed linens, then. Oh, and Mr. Hamilton, I'll have yer car brought around to the back, if you'd like. There's a rear entrance and a small service road that will take ye out to the main street. Nobody will notice if ye slip out that way."

"Thank you very much," Graeme said, dropping his car keys into her hand. "For everything."

"Val," Lara began doubtfully, after Margaret had left. "I'm not sure this is a good idea."

"I think it's a great idea." Graeme's tone said the issue had been resolved. He stood up. "Let's go upstairs and pack. We can be on the road in fifteen minutes."

"Do you mind if we eat your dinner?" Val asked, eyeing Lara's plate. "I'm actually a little hungry, come to think of it."

"Go right ahead." Lara stood up, casting Christopher an apologetic look. "I really am sorry about all of this."

He shrugged and slid into the booth opposite Valerie. "Don't worry about it. I know when I'm outgunned. Go on, get out of here."

Lara smiled her thanks at him, and then gave Valerie a hug. "Thank you so much," she whispered.

"No, thank you," Val said into her ear. "This is the most fun I've had in years."

Lara followed Graeme up the stairs. Two house-maids were in their room, putting fresh sheets on the bed and restocking the bathroom, working quickly and efficiently. After they left, Graeme pulled his duffel bag and Lara's suitcase out of the closet and began tossing their belongings into them.

"I'm sorry I got you into this," he finally said, closing her suitcase with a snap. "I never thought Tony would go this far. The good thing is that by this time next month, all of this will be old news and nobody will even remember anything."

"And what about you?" Lara asked quietly. "Will this be old news to you, too? Will you forget it ever happened?"

She wasn't talking about the salacious news story, and from the expression on his face, Graeme realized that. His eyes darkened and he took a step toward her.

"No. I'll remember everything. And if you're willing to give me a chance, I can show you that my life isn't all about signing autographs and doing interviews and running from the paparazzi."

Lara stilled. Her heart stopped beating and then exploded into life again. "What are you trying to say?"

Graeme blew out a hard breath, and in that instant Lara saw how difficult it was for him to open himself to her, to risk rejection or worse.

"I'm asking if you'll consider coming to New Zealand with me." He pressed a finger against her lips to stop her quick reply. "Before you answer, I should tell you that I'll be working on location, but it won't be every day. We'll still have plenty of time to be together. I'll have an apartment there, and I've heard some of the other cast are bringing their families, so you wouldn't be completely alone."

He withdrew his finger and Lara drew in a slow, steady breath. "What about the divorce papers?"

Graeme shrugged. "Bring them with you, if you must."

"What?"

"If I can't make you happy, then you still have your out. But I'd like more than just two days with you, love. You see, I haven't been able to put you in my past, and I'm still not convinced that what we shared wasn't just a fluke. I need more time to properly evaluate the situation."

"So you're saying that I should come with you, and if at any time you fail to make me happy then you'll sign the papers?"

"Well, not without doing my damndest to change your mind, of course," he said, grinning at her.

"Oh, Graeme," she breathed, feeling for the first time that her future might just hold everything that she'd ever dreamed about. But still, she hesitated. "I want to come with you, I really do."

"But—?"

"I can't leave for at least another month. The theater kids are doing a performance of *The Wizard of Oz,* and there's this one little girl… If I'm not there to see her—"

"Come when you're ready, then," he said, sliding his arms around her and pulling her against his chest. "I'll be waiting."

"Are you sure?"

"I want you to come with me more than I've wanted anything in my life, Lara."

"I want to be with you. Christopher can run the theater program without me. And it looks like Val will be happy to help him. But I do have a condition."

He pulled back to look at her. "What's that?"

"I'm not bringing the divorce papers. If you don't make me happy, then I'll let you know." She smiled at him. "I'm sure you can think of ways to get the relationship back on track."

"I'm certain I can," he agreed, his hands sliding over her back and drawing her closer. "But I can't promise it will always be easy going."

"We'll just need to work at it. Every day."

"And maybe twice a day, if I'm very lucky," he murmured, kissing her mouth.

"Mmm. I've decided to continue with my writing, but this time I'm going to shoot for publication. You can be my research assistant for the intimate scenes, but I should warn you that I may be very demanding."

"I should warn you that I'm a slow learner," he rasped against her lips. "You may need to show me things two or three times before I catch on."

"I'm very patient." Lara smiled.

Graeme smoothed her hair back from her face, studying her face as if he would commit each feature to memory. "I love you, Lara Hamilton, and I'm looking forward to a lifetime of research with you."

He was lowering his head toward hers when a female voice interrupted them.

"Hey, you two, if you want to avoid the reporters then you'd better go now while you can. The innkeeper said to tell you that the media are starting to arrive."

They drew apart to see Valerie and Christopher in the doorway of the room, each of them carrying a small overnight bag. Christopher looked anywhere but at them.

"I don't know about this, Val," he said dubiously, his

gaze traveling around their surroundings. "This room is pretty small, and there's only one bed."

Val gave Lara a knowing wink. "Oh, wow, I had no idea we'd have to *share a bed*. The things I do in the name of friendship."

Grinning, Graeme picked up his duffel bag and slung it over one shoulder before picking up Lara's small suitcase. "Thanks again for covering for us," he said to Christopher.

"Take care of her."

"I intend to." He wrapped his free arm around Lara's shoulder and drew her into the hallway where Margaret was waiting.

"There are reporters downstairs," she said quietly, "but I told them ye haven't left your room since ye arrived, that ye're like newlyweds." She smiled broadly. "Yer car is waiting in the back, and they'll never suspect a thing. Take this service staircase down to the first floor, turn left and then follow the corridor out to the rear entrance. Good luck, my dears."

Behind them, they heard Val's voice as she spoke to Christopher in a sultry tone. "Well, here we are, just you and me. You know, we could always work on our theater arts skills…maybe do a little role-playing to pass the time. So who do you prefer, Professor… Ginger or Mary Ann?"

They turned in time to see the bedroom door close, and then heard the lock as it clicked into place.

Lara turned to Graeme with a smile. "I always liked role-playing. After all, look how well it worked for me."

Graeme laughed and tucked her against his side as they made their way down the back staircase. "As much as I enjoyed your slave-girl performance, I like your current role best of all." He paused to kiss her. Softly. Reverently. "My wife."

Lara kissed him back, knowing it was a part she'd willingly keep for the rest of her life.

Epilogue

JOSIE UNLOCKED the door of the little costume shop, Dressed to Thrill, feeling unaccountably morose. Snow had fallen during the night, turning the Chicago streets into a glittering winter wonderland. Christmas was just weeks away, and she should be feeling more festive. The shop had never been busier and her boss, Carol, had just given birth to a healthy baby girl after a long and difficult pregnancy. She'd also promised Josie a nice Christmas bonus for running the shop while Carol had been on extended maternity leave. But instead of feeling jolly, Josie felt downright depressed. She'd be spending yet another holiday season alone.

She thought again of Tom, and mentally kicked herself for having been so rude to him the last time he'd come by the shop with a delivery, all because she'd overheard him talking to another woman on his cell phone. In retrospect, she'd behaved like an immature teenager. So what if he was seeing other women? She didn't have exclusive rights to him. She wasn't even dating him, for Pete's sake, and with an attitude like the one she'd displayed, she never would. How many times had her friends told her that she needed to show more confidence and be more assertive? She should have taken control of the situation and made her feelings clear. Instead, she'd let him walk out of the shop.

Closing the door behind her, Josie flipped on the lights and made her way to the stockroom at the back of the store, peeling off her hat and gloves as she went and shoving them into the pockets of her coat. It was still early, and the shop wouldn't open for another thirty minutes. She would put on a pot of coffee and watch the morning news while she went through the online orders.

Tossing her coat onto the sofa in the back room, she switched on the little television that sat on a shelf surrounded by brightly colored costume accessories. As she carefully measured out the coffee, she glanced at the television. The Chicago morning show was one of her favorites.

"And now, a very special story that's sure to warm even the coldest of hearts," said the smiling female talk-show host, "although ladies, if you're a Graeme Hamilton fan, this story might just break your heart."

Josie watched, intrigued, as the camera switched to a young couple standing in the middle of a bustling airport. Her eyes widened as she recognized Graeme Hamilton, the celebrity heartthrob from the television series *Galaxy's End*. He had one arm around a pretty redhead, and although he was talking to the reporter, his eyes never left the woman's face.

"So are the rumors true?" the reporter asked. "You're actually married, and you managed to keep it a secret for the past five years?"

"Yeah," Graeme said with a grin. "It's true. This is my wife, Lara."

Josie gasped, thinking of the online customer who had requested a *Galaxy's End* costume just a week earlier, and how she'd sent her a *Star Wars* costume instead. She hadn't switched the costumes to be malicious; she'd hoped to help the woman attract a man's attention, but apparently this man had never even been in the market. She recalled all the times she'd seen Graeme Hamilton's picture in the tabloids, escorting other women to movie premieres and promotional events. To think he'd been married all that time. Her opinion of him slid south, and she couldn't help but wonder what his wife thought about his keeping their marriage a secret.

"You're gorgeous," she murmured, "but not too bright."

The camera switched to the young woman, and Josie felt a pang of envy. Far from looking upset, she glowed with happiness. The woman was pretty in a wholesome, girl-next-door kind of way, but the expression in her blue eyes as she looked at Graeme made her downright beautiful. They were obviously nuts about each other.

"I just can't believe how everything worked out," the woman said, blushing as she caught Graeme's eye. "To think, I owe it all to a crazy costume mix-up."

Josie's mouth fell open. Setting the coffee down, she walked over to the television, her eyes riveted on the small screen.

"You see," Lara continued, smiling into her husband's eyes, "I always believed that our marriage ended five years ago. I had planned to attend the *Galaxy's End* fan festival to ask Graeme for a divorce. But then the costume shop sent me the wrong outfit, and when Graeme saw me at the masquerade ball—"

"I knew it was her right away," he interjected, his face close to hers. "We got married so young, and at the time it didn't work out." He shrugged. "We were just kids, and we had a lot of things working against us. But I never stopped loving her, and this time we're going to make it work."

Josie's eyes widened as Lara turned and looked directly into the camera. "I want to extend a special thank-you to the shop that mixed up my costume order, because without them I might not have my happy ending. So, to the people at Dressed to Thrill, if you're watching this, I just want to say thank-you. The costume you mistakenly sent made me feel confident and empowered. It gave me the courage to go after my dreams. And for the ladies out there, I know how disappointed you must be to find out that Graeme isn't single, but I promise you that there's a guy out there who's as perfect for you as he is for me."

The camera switched back to the morning show, where the talk-show hosts continued their animated discussion about Graeme and his surprise marriage, and they even ran a video clip of the outside of the costume shop. But Josie was no longer listening. She still couldn't believe how her deliberate costume mix-up had resulted in such a happy reunion.

Smiling, she drummed a finger against her lips. What had Lara said about having the courage to go after her dreams? Maybe that was the tactic she needed to use with Tom. The next time he showed up at her shop with a delivery, she'd confront him with her true feelings so that he was left in no doubt about how much she wanted him.

She just hoped the results would be as satisfying as Lara's....

* * * * *

*Celebrate 60 years of pure
reading pleasure with Harlequin®!
Just in time for the holidays,
Silhouette Special Edition® is proud
to present* New York Times
bestselling author Kathleen Eagle's
ONE COWBOY, ONE CHRISTMAS

Rodeo rider Zach Beaudry was a travelin' man—
until he broke down in middle-of-nowhere South
Dakota during a deep freeze. That's when an
angel came to his rescue....

blast of north wind. The right was his free arm anyway

"Don't die on me. Come on, Zel. You know how much I love you, girl. You're all I've got. Don't do this to me here. Not *now*."

But Zelda had quit on him, and Zach Beaudry had no one to blame but himself. He'd taken his sweet time hitting the road, and then miscalculated a shortcut. For all he knew he was a hundred miles from gas. But even if they were sitting next to a pump, the ten dollars he had in his pocket wouldn't get him out of South Dakota, which was not where he wanted to be right now. Not even his beloved pickup truck, Zelda, could get him much of anywhere on fumes. He was sitting out in the cold in the middle of nowhere. And getting colder.

He shifted the pickup into Neutral and pulled hard on the steering wheel, using the downhill slope to get her off the blacktop and into the roadside grass, where she shuddered to a standstill. He stroked the padded dash. "You'll be safe here."

But Zach would not. It was getting dark, and it was already too damn cold for his cowboy ass. Zach's battered body was a barometer, and he was feeling South Dakota, big time. He'd have given his right arm to be climbing into a hotel hot tub instead of a brutal blast of north wind. The right was his free arm anyway.

Damn thing had lost altitude, touched some part of the bull and caused him a scoreless ride last time out.

It wasn't scoring him a ride this night, either. A carload of teenagers whizzed by, topping off the insult by laying on the horn as they passed him. It was at least twenty minutes before another vehicle came along. He stepped out and waved both arms this time, damn near getting himself killed. Whatever happened to *do unto others?* In places like this, decent people didn't leave each other stranded in the cold.

His face was feeling stiff, and he figured he'd better start walking before his toes went numb. He struck out for a distant yard light, the only sign of human habitation in sight. He couldn't tell how distant, but he knew he'd be hurting by the time he got there, and he was counting on some kindly old man to be answering the door. No shame among the lame.

It wasn't like Zach was fresh off the operating table—it had been a few months since his last round of repairs—but he hadn't given himself enough time. He'd lopped a couple of weeks off the near end of the doc's estimated recovery time, rigged up a brace, done some heavy-duty taping and climbed onto another bull. Hung in there for five seconds—four seconds past feeling the pop in his hip and three seconds short of the buzzer.

He could still feel the pain shooting down his leg with every step. Only this time he had to pick the damn thing up, swing it forward and drop it down again on his own.

Pride be damned, he just hoped *somebody* would be answering the door at the end of the road. The light in the front window was a good sign.

The four steps to the covered porch might as well

have been four hundred, and he was looking to climb them with a lead weight chained to his left leg. His eyes were just as screwed up as his hip. Big black spots danced around with tiny red flashers, and he couldn't tell what was real and what wasn't. He stumbled over some shrubbery, steadied himself on the porch railing and peered between vertical slats.

There in the front window stood a spruce tree with a silver star affixed to the top. Zach was pretty sure the red sparks were all in his head, but the white lights twinkling by the hundreds throughout the huge tree, those were real. He wasn't too sure about the woman hanging the shiny balls. Most of her hair was caught up on her head and fastened in a curly clump, but the light captured by the escaped bits crowned her with a golden halo. Her face was a soft shadow, her body a willowy silhouette beneath a long white gown. If this was where the mind ran off to when cold started shutting down the rest of the body, then Zach's final worldly thought was, *This ain't such a bad way to go.*

If she would just turn to the window, he could die looking into the eyes of a Christmas angel.

* * * * *

Could this woman from Zach's past
get the lonesome cowboy to come in
from the cold...for good?
Look for
ONE COWBOY, ONE CHRISTMAS
by Kathleen Eagle
Available December 2009
from Silhouette Special Edition®

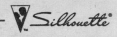

Silhouette Desire

FROM *NEW YORK TIMES* BESTSELLING AUTHOR

DIANA PALMER

THE MAVERICK

A BRAND-NEW LONG, TALL TEXAN STORY

Visit Silhouette Books at www.eHarlequin.com

SD76982

REQUEST YOUR FREE BOOKS!

2 FREE NOVELS PLUS 2 FREE GIFTS!

HARLEQUIN®

Blaze™

Red-hot reads!

YES! Please send me 2 FREE Harlequin® Blaze™ novels and my 2 FREE gifts (gifts are worth about $10). After receiving them, if I don't wish to receive any more books, I can return the shipping statement marked "cancel". If I don't cancel, I will receive 6 brand-new novels every month and be billed just $4.24 per book in the U.S. or $4.71 per book in Canada. That's a savings of 15% off the cover price. It's quite a bargain. Shipping and handling is just 50¢ per book.* I understand that accepting the 2 free books and gifts places me under no obligation to buy anything. I can always return a shipment and cancel at any time. Even if I never buy another book, the two free books and gifts are mine to keep forever.

151 HDN EYS2   351 HDN EYTE

Name _____ (PLEASE PRINT) _____

Address _____ Apt. # _____

City _____ State/Prov. _____ Zip/Postal Code _____

Signature (if under 18, a parent or guardian must sign) _____

Mail to the **Harlequin Reader Service:**
IN U.S.A.: P.O. Box 1867, Buffalo, NY 14240-1867
IN CANADA: P.O. Box 609, Fort Erie, Ontario L2A 5X3

Not valid to current subscribers of Harlequin Blaze books.

Want to try two free books from another line?
Call 1-800-873-8635 or visit www.morefreebooks.com.

* Terms and prices subject to change without notice. Prices do not include applicable taxes. N.Y. residents add applicable sales tax. Canadian residents will be charged applicable provincial taxes and GST. Offer not valid in Quebec. This offer is limited to one order per household. All orders subject to approval. Credit or debit balances in a customer's account(s) may be offset by any outstanding balance owed by or to the customer. Please allow 4 to 6 weeks for delivery. Offer available while quantities last.

Your Privacy: Harlequin Books is committed to protecting your privacy. Our Privacy Policy is available online at www.eHarlequin.com or upon request from the Reader Service. From time to time we make our lists of customers available to reputable third parties who may have a product or service of interest to you. If you would prefer we not share your name and address, please check here. ☐

HB09R3

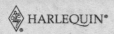

COMING NEXT MONTH

Available November 24, 2009

#507 BETTER NAUGHTY THAN NICE Vicki Lewis Thompson,
Jill Shalvis, Rhonda Nelson
A Blazing Holiday Collection
Bad boy Damon Claus is determined to mess things up for his jolly big brother,
Santa. Who'd ever guess that sibling rivalry would result in mistletoe madness
for three unsuspecting couples! And Damon didn't even have to spike the
eggnog....

#508 STARSTRUCK Julie Kenner
For Alyssa Chambers, having the perfect Christmas means snaring the
perfect man. And she has him all picked out. Too bad it's her best friend,
Christopher Hyde, who has her seeing stars.

#509 TEXAS BLAZE Debbi Rawlins
The Wrong Bed
Hot and heavy. That's how Kate Manning and Mitch Colter have always been for
each other. But it's not till Kate makes the right move—though technically in the
wrong bed—that things start heating up for good!

#510 SANTA, BABY Lisa Renee Jones
Dressed to Thrill, Bk. 4
As a blonde bombshell, Caron Avery thinks she's got enough attitude to bring a
man to his knees. But when she seduces hot playboy Baxter Remington, will she
be the one begging for more?

#511 CHRISTMAS MALE Cara Summers
Uniformly Hot!
All policewoman Fiona Gallagher wants for Christmas is a little excitement. But
once she finds herself working on a case with sexy captain D. C. Campbell,
she's suddenly aching for a different kind of thrill....

#512 TWELVE NIGHTS Hope Tarr
Blaze Historicals
Lady Alys is desperately in love with Scottish bad boy Callum Fraser. And
keeping him out of her bed until the wedding is nearly killing her. So what's
stopping them from indulging? Uhh...Elys's deceased first husband, a man very
much alive.

HBCNMBPA1109